HEART OF EON

EON WARRIORS #3

ANNA HACKETT

Heart of Eon

Published by Anna Hackett

Copyright 2019 by Anna Hackett

Cover by Melody Simmons of BookCoversCre8tive

Edits by Tanya Saari

ISBN (ebook): 978-1-925539-70-7

ISBN (paperback): 978-1-925539-71-4

Unexplored – Romantic Book of the Year
(Ruby) Novella Winner 2017

Unfathomed and Unmapped - Romantic Book
of the Year (Ruby) finalists 2018

At Star's End – One of Library Journal's Best
E-Original Romances for 2014

Return to Dark Earth – One of Library
Journal's Best E-Original Books for 2015 and
two-time SFR Galaxy Awards winner

The Phoenix Adventures – SFR Galaxy Award
Winner for Most Fun New Series and "Why
Isn't This a Movie?" Series

Beneath a Trojan Moon – SFR Galaxy Award Winner and RWAus Ella Award Winner

Hell Squad – SFR Galaxy Award for best Post-Apocalypse for Readers who don't like Post-Apocalypse

The Anomaly Series – #1 Amazon Action Adventure Romance Bestseller

"Like Indiana Jones meets Star Wars. A treasure hunt with a steamy romance." – SFF Dragon, review of *Among Galactic Ruins*

"Strap in, enjoy the heat of romance and the daring of this group of space travellers!" – Di, Top 500 Amazon Reviewer, review of *At Star's End*

"Action, danger, aliens, romance – yup, it's another great book from Anna Hackett!" – Book Gannet Reviews, review of *Hell Squad: Marcus*

Sign up for my VIP mailing list and get your *free box set* containing three action-packed romances.

Visit here to get started:
www.annahackettbooks.com

CHAPTER ONE

She crawled through the tight space, huffing and puffing.

God, she would give anything to be back in her cushy office, or her high-tech, decked-out computer lab. Anything was better than trying to squeeze her curvy ass through a vent tunnel on an alien warship.

An Eon warship that she'd hijacked.

Wren Traynor bumped her elbow against the tunnel wall and pain shot up her arm. She swallowed a curse and kept crawling. Then her knee scraped on something sharp and she barely swallowed a yelp. That was going to leave a bruise.

The things she did for her sisters.

Suddenly, a clanging sound echoed through the vent tunnel. She stopped, her heart jumping. She knew what that meant. The warriors were searching for her.

And they were getting close.

In the darkness, Wren pulled out her precious tablet and thumbed the screen. It flared to life.

Hmm, time to keep those big, brawny Eon warriors busy doing something else. Plus, get a little bit of enjoyment out of things. She deserved *some* fun since her life had gone to shit.

It had all started five months before, when her older sister, Eve, had been framed for a crime she didn't commit and locked away in a low orbit prison. *Dickwad Space Corps.* Eve had dedicated her life to the Corps, but they'd turned on her in an instant. Then, if that wasn't bad enough, Space Corps had blackmailed Eve into abducting an Eon war commander.

Bad idea. Wren's throat tightened, and she sent up a quick prayer that her sister was okay.

Things had gone from bad to worse when the Corps had approached Wren, offering to free Eve...but only if Wren hijacked an Eon warship, the *Rengard*, using her genius hacker skills.

Oh, and on top of that, the nasty insectoid aliens, the Kantos, were planning to invade and destroy Earth. Yep, her life was complete shit.

Wren sighed. She missed her cushy office and computer lab, she missed her apartment, and she missed her morning lattes. She sighed again. Earth needed the Eon Empire's help, sure, but she was totally unconvinced that abducting them and hijacking their warships was going to convince them to hold hands with Terrans and happily go into battle to save Earth.

Man, her life had definitely gone gurgling down the drain.

You're in over your head, Wren. The voice of her cheating, lying ex-boyfriend echoed in her head.

Smug bastard. She poked her tongue out. No way she was letting that asshole suck up any of her oxygen. She'd kicked his cheating ass out months ago, and even the echo of his voice wasn't welcome.

She tapped on the tablet screen, pulling up the schematics of the ship. Over the last few days, she'd been painstakingly mapping the *Rengard's* layout. Mostly so she could find out-of-the-way washrooms where she could relieve herself, and to keep one step ahead of the warriors.

Suddenly, a deep voice echoed through the tablet's speakers.

"Woman."

She rolled her eyes. War Commander Dann-Jad was a man of few words. Especially when he was angry.

"Good morning, WC," she said.

There was a pause. "WC?"

"War commander is a bit of a mouthful. Although, it's unfortunate that WC is an abbreviation for something *entirely* different on Earth."

There was a charged silence. Wren could practically feel the *Rengard's* war commander reining in his temper.

"Return full control of my ship to me. Now."

Here we go again. She lowered her voice to match his. "You silly Terran woman, return control of my ship to me. I've asked you dozens of times, and every time you've said no, but I'll try again." Wren let her voice return to normal. "Screw you, WC. I've got a planet to save, and a sister to rescue."

And her mission was to get the *Rengard* to a rendezvous point, where they would meet the Space Corps.

She still was uncertain as to how Space Corps thought they were going to subdue Dann-Jad and his fully trained warriors. The Eon warriors, although they shared the same ancestor with the people of Earth, were taller, bigger, stronger, and generally more badass.

Oh, and bonded to a kickass alien symbiont that gave them the ability to create cool armor and weapons with a mere thought.

Of course, during their game of cat and mouse, Dann-Jad had disabled the ship's star drive. That meant they were crawling along at regular, old thruster speed. The journey would take weeks.

And Wren's food supply was dangerously low. She'd run out of chocolate and coffee days ago. Her body was crying out for caffeine. Her rations were down to some freeze-dried disgustingness masquerading as chicken stew and cardboard-flavored nutrition bars. *Blergh.*

Not to mention she smelled bad. She sniffed herself and winced. She'd used her last wet wipe hours ago. She was moving well beyond the desperate need for a shower, and while she risked using the washrooms tucked deep in the bowels of the ship to relieve herself, she didn't dare spend any more time in there. That was all she needed, getting caught with her spacesuit around her ankles by the war commander.

Luckily, I love my sisters. She felt a pang of emotion, hoping, praying Eve and Lara were both okay. Lara had to be so worried.

"Wren Traynor," Dann-Jad growled, "As I told you before, the Eon now have an alliance with Earth—"

"Lies. You're trying to trick me."

"War commanders do not lie or trick." He really sounded pissed now.

"I've got things to do." She stabbed the button on her tablet to stop their little tête-à-tête.

She started crawling again, banged her shoulder, and cursed loudly. She turned a corner, and knew she was close to the *Rengard's* engine room. Scanning the metal wall, she found the maintenance panel she was looking for.

"A-ha." She pulled out her AllDriver and quickly worked the panel off. Then she lifted her tablet, tapping into the *Rengard's* systems. It was a risk, because if the warriors caught her in there, they could pinpoint her location. She tapped on the screen, her fingers flying as she activated the program she'd been working on. She *needed* to get the star drives back online.

She tapped again. *Yes. Got it.*

The vent tunnel vibrated beneath her. She wiggled her booty. "Yes!"

As the engines spooled up, she imagined War Commander Dann-Jad sitting in his cushy office near the bridge, calling her lots of names.

Time to go. She tapped the controls and initiated a jump to light speed that would send them closer to Earth. For a second, it felt like the air around her blurred.

She knew they were now rushing along at the speed of light.

Then suddenly, the ship jolted. Wren's forehead

smacked the side of the tunnel. *Jesus.* Rubbing her head, she felt the speed drop away and the vibrations of the engines die.

Damn the man! She screeched and thumped her hand against the wall. Pain radiated up her arm. "Ow."

"You are not hijacking my ship," Dann-Jad's voice came from her tablet again.

He'd hacked her tablet again. Damn, whoever his hacker was, they were good.

"I already have, WC."

She heard his growl. "I'll make you regret your actions."

Too late. She already did.

Wren dragged in a breath. Well, now it was time to keep her war commander busy. So busy, in fact, he wouldn't have time to stop her the next time she got the star drives back online. She swiped her screen, her tongue between her teeth.

There. She grinned and imagined his face. *How do you like that, WC?*

Oh yeah, the small pleasures. It paid to take them when she could find them.

She heard another vicious growl through the tablet, and she could almost imagine him with cartoon steam pouring out his ears.

Now, time to get those star drives working again. Wren started crawling.

WITH A GROWL, War Commander Malax Dann-Jad

tugged at the collar of his black uniform. The high-tech fabric was damp with sweat, and perspiration sheened his bare arms.

"Airen!"

His second appeared in the doorway of his office. She was also sweating.

"War commander." Her brown hair was pulled back in a braid, and a few strands were stuck to her damp forehead.

"Status of the ventilation on the bridge level."

"We're still working on it."

Cren. How could one small Terran woman cause all this upheaval?

Malax slammed his fist against his desk. Second Commander Airen Kann-Felis didn't flinch, but the woman's black-green eyes moved to stare at the wall. She'd been his second-in-command long enough to know to ignore his bursts of temper.

"Work harder." The helian symbiont circling Malax's wrist pulsed, reacting to his emotions.

"The Terran has scrambled several systems. The team is doing everything they can." Airen released a breath. "Malax, if we can pump some *daros* gas into the ventilation system—"

"No. She is not to be harmed and I can't risk the gas getting into the rest of the ship."

"It wouldn't kill her."

"Are you an expert on Terran physiology, Airen?"

His second sighed. "No."

"Find another way."

"Yes, sir." Airen pursed her lips, swiveled, and left.

For days, his ship had been under Wren Traynor's control. Lights had been going out, they'd had ventilation problems, and she'd had them jumping all around the Syrann Quadrant before he'd managed to shut down the star drives.

His warriors still couldn't find her, and they'd been searching every maintenance conduit, ventilation tunnel, and storage closet for days.

He pulled in a ragged breath. Malax liked control. Being a war commander was in his blood. He'd been born for the job, like his father before him.

By Alqin's axe, he *would* take back his ship.

He touched the comp screen on his desk, and a picture of Wren Traynor appeared. He stared at her face. She was flanked by her sisters in the image. According to the partial transmissions he'd managed to receive from the *Desteron*, both of Wren's sisters were now, unbelievably, mated to Eon warriors and safe aboard the other warship.

He'd tried sending the transmissions to Wren as proof, but she hadn't let the files through and accused him of trying to implant a bug in her tablet.

His gaze fell on the image again. Wren's sisters were far taller than her. Eve Traynor had managed to abduct the most decorated war commander in the Eon fleet right off his ship. Somehow, after an attack by the Kantos, Eve and Davion Thann-Eon had ended up mated. And then Lara Traynor, after stealing several sacred Eon gems, had ended up mated to the warrior sent to track her down— Davion's security commander, Caze Vann-Jad.

With the Kantos looming, Earth had gotten desperate. One part of Malax understood. The Kantos were ruthless and unforgiving. The bug-like beings swarmed planets, decimating everything in their path. In a risky move, Earth's Space Corps had sent the Traynor sisters to kidnap, steal, and hijack as a way to gain the Eon Empire's attention.

The plan, Malax admitted dryly, had worked.

He looked at Wren's face. She was different from her sisters. The older two were clearly athletic, and both had harder, tougher lines on their faces that said they were used to command and combat. Both were a part of Earth's Space Corps—Eve, a Sub Captain, and Lara, a special forces marine.

Wren was shorter, smaller, and softer looking. It was clear she laughed a lot just from looking at her face.

Malax had grown up with sisters. He had four of them. And after his father had died, Malax had become his family's provider, their protector. So, he knew how to deal with females.

But Wren Traynor was eroding the last of his patience.

His ship was in disarray and at risk. And only his top-level warriors knew, but the *Rengard* had some top-secret, experimental technology buried in the heart of its systems.

Tech he knew their enemies would kill to get their hands on.

Without full control of his ship, any enemy could move in on them. Malax gripped the edge of his desk. It was his responsibility to keep his ship, its tech, and its warriors safe. His gut hardened, old memories bombarding his head. His helian pulsed again.

He pulled in a deep breath. He would *not* lose any of his warriors. Not again.

Once again, he touched his comp, trying to contact her. The warriors on his communications team had done outstanding work to allow him to access her system. Not full access, and not enough to find where she was hiding, but enough to communicate with her.

"Wren Traynor." He stared at the blinking screen, waiting for an answer. "Woman, respond."

"I'm *busy*."

He frowned at the tart response. "Busy destroying my ship."

"God, you're moody."

Malax gritted his teeth so hard he heard a cracking sound in his jaw. "You've hijacked my ship, making it and my warriors vulnerable—"

"I'm too busy to talk right now, WC. Take a chill pill, and we can do some verbal sparring later."

The comm link went dead.

Malax wanted to throw something at the wall. Digging deeper than ever for some control, he sat back in his chair, tugging at his collar. He was angry, hot, and cranky.

And one tiny, Terran woman was to blame.

CHAPTER TWO

M alax felt the telltale rumble of the star drives coming online.

The bridge exploded into movement and voices.

"She's got the star drives back up," a warrior said.

"Can anyone pinpoint her location?" another yelled.

"Get the drives offline," Malax barked. "Now!"

As he watched his team scramble, Malax stared out the window, watching as the stars moved into long lines as they picked up speed. Wily woman. He had to admit he felt a grudging respect for Wren's smarts and persistence.

For decades after first contact, the Eon had believed that the Terrans of Earth were inferior. Lacking both intelligence and discipline.

The Traynor sisters were changing that viewpoint.

He watched his engineers scrambling, swiping at their screens.

"Where is she?" he asked his security commander.

Sabin Solann-Ath's eyes were almost all black, with only a few threads of purple. The stoic warrior had a sense of stillness that always made Malax think of a predator hunting prey.

Sabin shook his head. "She has to be close to the engine room."

Another security team member nodded. "I've got a rough location. It's not exact, but she's definitely bow-side of the engine room. In the maintenance conduits."

Malax swiveled, running out the door of the bridge. His boots thudded on the black metal floor as he powered down the corridor. He ignored the turbo lift—he didn't want to chance his little hijacker trapping him in there. Instead, he took an access ladder down to the engine-room level.

When he burst into the engine room, his engineering team looked up at him with startled looks on their faces.

Ignoring them, he pushed toward the far wall of the engine room. He heard and felt the engines hit max capacity. But Malax had been on starships his entire life, and the increased speed barely affected his balance. His gaze honed in on the wall.

She was in there. Somewhere. *Where was she taking them?*

He had to convince the woman that they were now on the same side, before some enterprising enemy saw the *Rengard* drifting around and acting erratically, and decided she'd make easy prey.

He scanned the wall, and his gaze fell on the cover for a maintenance conduit. He strode over to it, and one of the young engineering warriors nearby straightened.

"War commander—"

Malax barged past the man. He gripped the conduit cover and wrenched it off. Behind it was a narrow, horizontal tunnel, far too small for him to enter. In these small conduits, they had autonomous bots that carried out the necessary maintenance. He bent and peered inside. His pulse jumped.

He spotted her at the end of the tunnel. Startled, her head shot up. She ripped her tablet out of a connection on the wall.

Then, the brazen little Terran lifted a hand and waved at him. "Hey there, WC."

"Wren Traynor. I don't suppose you'll hand yourself over to me?"

She tossed her mass of curly hair back over her shoulder, then tapped a finger against her jaw. "Um...no."

He looked back at the young engineer hovering nearby. "Get a laser cutter here. Now."

The man hurried away.

When Malax looked back, Wren was smiling at him.

"You look as grumpy in real life as you sound in your messages."

And she looked more beautiful than he'd imagined. The thought made him curse in his head. He scowled at her. "You have—"

Suddenly, the ship jerked to a rapid halt. Malax was almost knocked off his feet, and slammed his palms against the wall to stay upright.

His team had managed to shut down the star drives.

At the end of the conduit tunnel, he saw Wren tumble over. Her head smacked against the wall.

"Wren!"

She held a hand to her head and looked dazed.

"Wren!"

She rubbed her temple. "I'm okay. Looks like you guys shut me down again."

The engineer returned, holding a set of laser cutters. Malax waved him forward, and the man flicked the tool on. A blue flame shot out the end of the long device. He started cutting into the wall.

Wren's lips quirked. "Looks like it's time for me to go. By the way, while I was in your system, I found that it is *waaaaay* too easy to hack into your navigation systems. That would be bad if you had enemies aboard."

"You aren't an enemy?"

She winked. "Nope. Otherwise I would have ejected you and your warriors into space days ago. Anyway, you might want to plug that hole before somebody not as nice as me finds it."

Malax wanted to get his hands on her and drag her out of there. He leaned in. "Wren—"

She lifted her palm and blew Malax a kiss.

Then she slid out of view. *Gone.*

He thumped a fist into the wall, making the young engineer jump.

"Don't bother with the cutters," Malax said. "Set up surveillance in these tunnels to make sure she can't get back in."

The engineer nodded. "Yes, sir."

Malax swiveled and strode out of the engine room. When he made it back to the bridge, he started barking orders. All around, his warriors stared at him from their consoles.

"Airen, get a team to check the navigation system for any weaknesses."

His second frowned. "Why?"

"Wren said she found a problem."

"And you trust her?"

"Just check it."

Airen nodded. "On it."

"Sabin, find that Terran."

Sabin's cool face hardened. "We'll find her. She will regret her course of action."

Malax stared at his security commander. "She is not to be harmed."

Sabin frowned. "Sir—"

"That's an order, Sabin."

The warrior released a breath and nodded, then stalked out of Malax's office.

Malax dropped into his chair, turning to stare out the window. If this kept up, his second and security command would stage a mutiny.

Where was Wren now? He knew she had to be running out of food, and they'd been carefully monitoring the ship's supplies.

When she'd first hijacked his ship, she'd been an enemy. One that he'd wanted to neutralize.

Now he knew she wasn't the enemy, just a misguided sister trying to take care of her family and save her planet. Malax understood the driving need to protect those you cared about.

But he wanted his ship back, and he needed Wren Traynor contained before she hurt herself.

Airen appeared in the doorway. Her toned arms were bare, her hair still in a braid, and he found himself thinking of Wren's differences—her wild curls and curvy body.

"She was right," Airen said. "We found a security gap in the navigation system."

Malax pulled in a breath. "Fix it. Airen, any signs of unfriendlies on long-range scans?"

"Nothing yet." Airen's lips firmed. "But we've been lucky no one's targeted the *Rengard* yet. We're far from Eon space, flying erratically, sometimes stopped. Someone's going to notice."

That's what Malax was afraid of. And he was responsible for the lives of every warrior on board, and for the advanced, top-secret tech onboard.

As his second left, he looked out of the window again. One small woman had evaded his entire crew for days. What the *cren* was he going to do about Wren Traynor?

———

WREN FOUND another spot to tap back into the *Rengard's* systems. It was masked by some low-level energy signatures from the engine room. But despite her best efforts, she couldn't bring the star drives back online.

Crapola. She slammed her tablet against her knees and wrinkled her nose. Dann-Jad had some good people on his team. When she'd headed off on this mission, she'd made the assumption that Eon warriors were all brawn, hard muscles, and handsome faces. And at first, she'd thought they looked identical too—similar rugged features, brown hair, mostly black eyes with filaments of color.

Then she thought of the war commander's face and her pulse jumped.

He seemed a little more handsome, his cheekbones a little sharper, his hair a shade darker. Sex on a stick.

She scrubbed a hand over her eyes. God, what was it with her and handsome men? Lance, the dastardly cheating ex, had been model handsome. As the owner of a gym, he'd worked out all the time, had the body of a god...and liked to screw tight-bodied, yoga instructors in the backroom.

Bastard. Anyway, she so should *not* be lusting over a man right now. Especially not the one who wanted to wring her neck and probably toss her out an airlock.

And especially not when she smelled so bad. She sniffed herself and shook her head.

Well, she had no star drives...so, she needed another plan of attack.

Then a thought hit her. She smiled. The war commander would be busy in his office off the bridge for the next few hours. She'd made a habit of noting his movements, and the man was a workaholic.

If he was busy, she was going to have a shower.

Wren climbed through the vents, heading upward toward the ship's cabins. She checked her schematics a few times. When this was over, she was going to have an extremely accurate layout of all the *Rengard's* vents and conduits.

Huffing a little, she neared the upper levels. Then her tablet beeped.

Pausing, she frowned. There was a super-weird energy signature coming from right beside her. She studied the conduit layout, and realized there was a small room in there. *Hmm.* She couldn't see a way into the space.

What were the Eon hiding in there? The energy signature didn't appear to be dangerous. She shrugged. Regardless of what it was, this could be a good little hidey-hole for her. The warriors were getting way too close to the small space that she'd used as a home base for the last few days.

Wren tapped her screen and made a note.

But right now, she only had one priority. She kept crawling, and finally moved down a horizontal vent duct. She stopped, checked her tablet, and smiled.

Running her fingers over the panels, she pried one open and looked down. Into a large, neat cabin. *Perfect.*

Wren slipped her legs through the hole, gripping the edge. Hmm, climbing down into the cabin wasn't quite as easy as she imagined. She felt one of the panels bow under her weight. Dammit, these vent tunnels weren't built to hold much weight.

Eve and Lara would leap down athletically, like a panther or something. Or maybe they'd somersault in, like a...somersaulter. Was somersaulter even a word?

With a roll of her eyes, Wren lowered herself down, her legs dangling ungracefully and her arms burning. Then her hand slipped and she fell. *Shit.* She dropped the last meter and a half, and smacked onto the floor.

"Oof." She turned onto her back, the wind knocked out of her. She stared up at the hole she'd just fallen through. Yep, *so* not like her sisters.

She sat up and glanced around. Damn, War Commander Dann-Jad had a *nice* cabin.

It was spacious for a warship, and orderly, of course. She was pretty sure that man wouldn't let *anything* in his life get out of order. There were no personal touches, and the bed was neatly made.

Rising, she unrepentantly snooped around. She pulled open drawers and looked in the closet. It was filled with massive, warrior-sized uniforms. They were all black, and hung with military precision. She stroked the cover on his bed and tested his pillows. *Nice.* She expected them to be rock-hard, but they were soft. A nice fragrance hit her. A woodsy scent, with a touch of crisp citrus. She realized it was the war commander's scent and dropped the pillow.

Okay, enough snooping. Shower.

She made her way to the adjacent washroom and almost moaned. It wasn't big, but Wren would stand naked in a crocodile-infested river if it meant she could get clean. She set her tablet down and stripped off her smelly clothes, and this time she did moan. She spotted a clothes cleaner on the wall and opened the drawer. She shoved the high-tech spacesuit Space Corp had given her and her panties inside. Hopefully, the Eon tech would work on her clothes and not destroy them.

Once the clothes cleaner was operational, she stepped into the shower stall. When she turned on the shower, her belly fluttered. Warm, misty water hit her.

Now she groaned, long and loud. She didn't care that the shower had a water-saving device that made it more mist than actual water. She used the war commander's liquid soap, which unsurprisingly smelled like his pillow. She washed her hair twice, then scrubbed her skin all over.

For a second, she imagined the war commander in the stall. Naked. Water running over his dark-bronze skin. His big shoulders taking up all the space.

A shiver went through her.

Now is not the time, Wren. Reluctantly, she turned the water off, and then grabbed a giant, warrior-sized, drying cloth. She rubbed herself down, then wrapped the cloth around herself several times.

She let out a long breath. *Clean.* It felt so damn good.

Moving over to the clothes cleaner, she saw the cycle was almost finished. Idly, she picked up her tablet.

And squeaked.

Dann-Jad's signature was moving. *Toward his cabin.*

Shit, shititty, shit.

She yanked open the unfinished clothes cleaner and pulled her spacesuit out.

The fabric was still hot. "Ouch, ouch."

She flapped the suit to cool it off. Where were her panties? *Screw it.* No time. She shoved her leg into the spacesuit. Hopping from one foot to the other, she got it up to her hips, where it got tight.

Ugh. She shimmied and wriggled. The fabric finally moved upward and she slipped her arms in. As she did up the central fastening, she was grateful it had a built-in bra support. She had no desire for her girls to be on the loose. She shoved her feet back into her boots.

She glanced at her tablet and her stomach clenched. Oh, God, he was almost there.

She raced back into the cabin. When she looked up at the hole in the ceiling, she realized she had no idea how the hell she was going to get back up there.

Think, Wren, think. She leaped onto Malax's bed and bounced a few times.

Taking a deep breath, she bounced and leaped for the hole.

Her fingers brushed the edge but she missed. She landed back on the war commander's bed on her knees.

With a curse, she rose. The bed covers were in complete disarray. *Sorry, WC.* She eyed the hole again. With a huge bounce, she managed to catch the edge. Yes! Heaving and straining, she pulled herself upward...and managed to *donk* her forehead on the edge.

Ow. Ignoring the bump, she climbed into the vent tunnel, just as she heard the cabin door chime below.

Shit. Quickly, she shoved the cover over the vent hole. Then she lay there, her heart pounding so hard it felt like it was about to burst out of her chest.

She heard heavy footsteps below.

Wren bit her lip. That was close. *Too* close.

Then she heard a deep, muffled curse.

She grinned. He was probably taking in his wrecked bed.

A groaning sound. Like metal moving on metal. *What?* Then the cover beneath Wren gave way, and with a cry, she fell.

CHAPTER THREE

Ceiling panels rained down on Malax's head. Then he heard a startled cry.

The next second, he caught a small, curvy female in his arms, and he looked into pretty blue eyes.

Wren's eyes widened and then, without warning, she pulled her fist back and punched him in the face.

Cren. As pain exploded through Malax's nose, his arms loosened, and he dropped her.

Her feet hit the floor and she scuttled away, rounding the bed to put it between them.

Malax took in both her and his cabin. The bed covers were mussed, and he saw a wet drying cloth in a pile near his washroom door.

He'd been trying to find her for days, and here she was in his cabin. Apparently...bathing?

"Stay back, War Commander." She held up a tablet and brandished it like a weapon.

"Oh, no." He shook his head. "Now that I have you, I'm not letting you get away."

"Remember, none of this is personal. Me hijacking your warship...it isn't what I wanted to do. My sisters—"

"Are safe. And both of them are happily mated to Eon warriors."

Wren's eyes bugged out of her head. "What?" Her voice turned to a screech.

"Eve mated with Davion, War Commander Thann-Eon."

Wren looked at Malax for a second, blinked, then bent over laughing. She laughed so hard that tears tracked down her cheeks.

"Wow, you're a terrible liar," she said.

Frustration welled in Malax's chest. "I'm not lying."

"Whoa." She pressed a hand to her chest. "I can *feel* the emotion pumping off you."

"Yes. My helian amplifies my emotions."

Her gaze dropped to the thick band around his wrist that housed his symbiont. Then she shook her head. "Look, there is no way that my sister Eve is mated to an Eon warrior." She shook her head. "Nuh-uh. Not possible."

"And Lara, as well," he continued.

More laughing. He even heard her snort. "Lara is back on Earth."

"No. Space Corps sent her into Eon space to try and steal our sacred gems. She mated with the warrior sent to track her down."

Wren laughed harder.

Malax tapped his boot on the floor and crossed his

arms over his chest. As she laughed, he let his gaze drift over her. He'd seen pictures of her, but it hadn't quite prepared him for the full impact of her curvy body in her tight, black-and-white spacesuit. Or the abundance of curls still drying around her shoulders.

"Wren, return control of my ship to me."

She blew out a breath, putting her hands on her hips. "I can't."

"Our planets have an alliance. I have transmissions from your sisters—"

"Transmissions can be faked."

He growled. How the *cren* could he get through to her? "You're putting everyone on this ship at risk. My warriors only have limited control of the ship's systems, including weapons. If we come across any enemies..." He let that thought hang.

She swallowed. "And my entire planet, not to mention the two people I love most, are in danger. I can't, I'm sorry."

"I am, too." Malax lunged for her.

But she was quick. She darted to the left, then leaped onto his bed, running across it. On the other side she grabbed his small bedside lamp, unclicked it from the latch holding it to the table, and threw it at him.

As he ducked, she raced for the door. He leaped over the bed and cut her off. She dodged to the right, her hip smacking into his built-in desk. She grabbed a small box from the desk and tossed it at him. He caught it and threw it aside.

She ran again, and as she was about to jump over his bed again, he snaked an arm out. He caught her around the waist and yanked her back against him. She twisted and struggled wildly.

Malax was trying desperately not to hurt her. She was so small, and he was more than aware that he was far bigger and stronger than she was.

He spun her around, and she made a choked noise. Then she lifted her knee, ramming it between his legs.

He swiveled at the last second and her knee rammed into his thigh. Hard.

At least she'd missed her original target. Still, he grunted, and his leg gave out. They tumbled onto the bed.

More wrestling. She kicked and flailed. *Enough of this*. He rolled and pinned her beneath him.

They both went still.

Cren. His hips fell between her open legs, and their bodies pressed together. She smelled good. He breathed deep, and realized it was the scent of his own soap on her hair. She felt good, too. So soft.

Blue eyes went wide. Her hair was tangled around her face, and she looked winded. Then she lifted a hand, her fingers brushing down his cheek.

It was such a small touch, and yet Malax felt it all the way through his body, right to his hardening cock.

"What are you doing to me?" he growled as he lowered his head until their lips were a whisper apart.

"I have no idea," she murmured. "But you're doing it to me, too."

He shifted, which only succeeded in pressing his stiff cock harder into her body. They both groaned.

"God, stop," she said. "I can't have you mesmerizing me like this."

25

He blinked. "Wren—"

"Sorry, you are gorgeous and all, but I took a vow to steer clear of guys like you."

"Guys like me?"

"Big, muscled, ripped."

Ripped? He frowned at her.

"Not to mention guys who want to lock me in their brig. So, I have to do this." She shifted her other hand, and he felt her slap her tablet against his shoulder.

An electric shock ran through his body.

Gritting his teeth, Malax's body shuddered. His muscles locked tight, none of his limbs under his control.

He managed to meet those blue eyes and he thought he saw regret in them.

"It's a localized charge I designed for close quarters combat." She bit her lip. "I'm really, really sorry, WC."

WREN HEAVED AND FINALLY, on attempt number three, succeeded in rolling the war commander's prone body off her. He flopped onto the bed beside her.

She sat up, her skin tingling and her belly fluttering. God, she'd just stunned an Eon war commander.

If he was pissed before...

She looked down at him. Her gaze started at the heavy boots on his feet and skimmed up the black trousers covering his long legs. Damn, the man had big, muscular thighs. She skimmed over the bulge she'd just felt pressed between her thighs, her throat going dry. His black, sleeveless shirt was suction tight, and she could see

26

the outline of all the ridges of his cut abdomen under the fabric. *Hell.* His body was unreal. No one should have that many abs. He made Lance look like a couch potato. She moved her attention up over his chest and his bulging biceps.

Wow. Just...wow.

She reached out and stroked his arm, her gaze moving upward. Her eyes locked with his. She jolted. He was *still* conscious and watching her. With furious eyes.

"You're sure easy to look at." *And apparently, I have a weakness for good-looking, fit men.* Her cheeks were flaming, but she could hardly hide the fact she'd been blatantly checking him out.

He glared at her.

Right. He was all cut perfection and warrior discipline. And she was...not cut. And not very disciplined. Wren was sure he preferred statuesque, warrior-woman types. Like her sisters.

Hello, Wren. Get out of there before he can move again. He should be out cold from the shock she'd given him. She shifted, getting ready to leave, when her gaze fell on the helian circling around his thick wrist. *Fascinating.* Curious, she touched it and felt a pulse of warmth from it. *Whoa.*

"Look—" she forced herself back to the matter at hand "—I need to get the *Rengard* to the meeting point with the Space Corps. I don't want anyone to get hurt." Her nose wrinkled. "Well, any more than they already have. I am sorry about the stunning thing." She eyed him. "I can feel your angry thoughts battering at me."

27

It was true. His emotions practically filled the room. It was a weird feeling.

She patted his chest and then slid off the bed. Her eyes went to the damaged panel in the ceiling above her. God, she was going to have to climb up there *again*.

Well, she couldn't bounce on the bed this time, because the giant, stunned warrior was sprawled on it.

Glancing around, she grabbed a chair from the desk and dragged it over. She climbed up, then jumped for the hole.

She missed. *Shit*. She tried a few more times, trying to grip the edge. Soon, she was out of breath. This entire situation was made worse by the fact that Malax was watching her ungraceful attempts to escape.

Finally. She grabbed the edge of the vent tunnel and pulled herself up. She checked her tablet was safe in her pocket, then dropped her head down through the hole. She looked at Malax upside down.

"Catch you later, War Commander."

He shot her another furious glare, just as alarms started blaring.

Startled, she jerked, thumping her shoulder on the side of the hole. *Ouch*. Damn, did the *Rengard's* warriors know what she'd done to their war commander?

Best not to stick around to find out. *Time to go*. With one last glance at the furious alien warrior sprawled on the bed, she ducked back into the vent tunnel.

Time to get, while the getting was good.

THE EFFECTS of the stun slowly wore off, and Malax sat up with a curse. *By Alqin's axe*, that Terran was infuriating, surprising, and annoying.

Shaking his head to clear it, he touched his communicator. The ship's alarms were still blaring and he needed to find out what was going on. "Report."

Airen's calm voice came across the line. "I've been trying to reach you. We have Kantos on scanners."

Malax swallowed another curse. "Are they attacking?"

"No. They're still too far away, but they're interested."

"Cut the alarms, but keep the ship on alert. Monitor the Kantos. I'll be on the bridge shortly."

"Malax, we need full control of the ship," his second said. "We only have limited weapons' control."

"I know. I'll take care of it."

He stood slowly, testing his limbs, his hands finally going to his hips. The *Rengard* was just sitting there, floating in space. A big target for the Kantos, or any other enemies who wanted to get their hands on a high-tech Eon warship.

He looked around his cabin. It was a mess. He strode across the space, searching for any clue that Wren might have left behind. He glanced at the broken ceiling panels and made a mental note to have maintenance fix them. Then, he spotted something in the washroom, hanging off the corner of his clothes cleaner.

He strode over and grabbed the silky scrap of fabric. He held it up and his gut hardened.

It was a tiny pair of women's panties. He studied the

scrap of pink lace, and then, against his better judgement, he shoved them in his pocket.

Striding out of his cabin, he marched down the corridor and touched his communicator.

"Wren?"

"The alarms stopped," her voice came through clearly. "I'm assuming everything's okay?"

"No, everything is not okay. The Kantos are in range."

He heard her hiss across the line.

"I need control of my ship, Wren. I need engines and weapons. We need to get out of here."

There was a pause. "I'll give you weapons."

He growled. "Wren, I'm not tricking you. Your sisters are safe and mated. The Eon have an alliance with Earth—"

"People lie all the time, Malax. And then they let you down."

He frowned. Who had done that to her?

"Look," she said. "I am really sorry about stunning you."

"What about almost kissing me?"

Now a strangled sound came across the line. "*You* almost kissed *me*. And you rubbed yourself up against me!"

"You appeared to enjoy it."

"Don't make fun of me."

He frowned. "I'm not—"

"Just stop talking."

"It also appeared you enjoyed messing up my cabin. "

A pause. "Well, I'm a little sorry about that."

"Just a little?"

"Look, I've got to go, WC."

The line went dead, and again, he wondered where she was, if she was okay, if she was hungry. Malax shook his head, continuing on his way to the bridge.

Here he was, the famed War Commander Dann-Jad, worrying about a small, Terran woman who'd hijacked his ship, when he should be worried about his warriors and his warship.

Time to focus on his *cren*-cursed job.

CHAPTER FOUR

W ren was sick of crawling. She turned a corner into yet another tunnel and kept moving.

At least she was clean.

And it was kind of a bonus that she got to rub up against a hot guy.

Her skin flushed. She'd never anticipated this reaction to an Eon war commander. She wondered what exactly Malax did to have so many muscles.

Quit daydreaming, Wren. After Lance, she was well aware that her taste in men was off. Her sisters hadn't liked Lance from day one, but Wren hadn't seen it. She'd been so flattered that he'd been interested in her, and the sex had been pretty good. It had taken catching him doing a long-limbed, naked yoga instructor on his office desk for her to see the truth. *I needed something you couldn't give me, babe.* What an asshole. He'd always made snide remarks about her: her body, her intelligence, her bank balance. She'd earned way more than him and he hadn't liked it. God, she was so stupid to fall for it.

Shaking her head, she checked her tablet. She'd retrieved her mostly empty backpack and was moving back toward the room with the energy signature. She really hoped it would be a good little hiding place to hole up.

Her thoughts turned to the Kantos. Damn alien bugs. She hated that they were close. She needed to give control of the ship back to Malax. No way she'd risk the lives of everyone on board for Space Corps' little game of galactic chess.

She paused. Was it possible that Eve and Lara were really mated to Eon warriors? That Earth had an alliance with the Eon Empire?

Eve and Lara mated? Wren shook her head at the idea. No way.

Neither of her sisters had ever had much time for men. Both were dedicated to their careers—or Eve had been, before her imprisonment. When her sisters had taken up with a guy, they both kept it simple, with no ties.

Wren kept crawling, frustration building when she felt the vent tunnel shift upward. She groaned.

Grunting and huffing, she pulled herself upward, and then finally she was alongside the strange energy signature. She searched the vent walls until she found a panel. She pulled out her AllDriver. With a few whizzes, the screws were undone, and the panel came loose.

Blue light flooded into the vent shaft.

Whoa. She quickly squeezed her way inside, and found there was enough space for her to stand.

She rose. *Double whoa.* The circular space wasn't huge, and all around the walls, glowing blue crystals were set into the wall. There were big ones—almost as big as she was—and small ones that would fit in the palm of her hand. In the center of the space was a small table, and in the middle of it was a growth of blue crystals that made her think of the kiddie crystal experiments she'd loved to grow when she was little.

Walking closer, she reached out and stroked one of the large crystals on the wall. A shadow moved inside it and she snatched her hand back.

What the hell?

More shadows moved within the crystals and her heart thumped. With a start, she realized what it was— helians. *Oh, wow.* Somehow, the Eon had embedded their symbionts into the *Rengard's* systems.

This was fascinating. She'd never heard of anything like this before. She lifted her tablet, scanning the room. The helians obviously played some important role in the ship's systems. Thoughts raced through her head as she imagined the possibilities. Man, what she wouldn't give to be able to research this.

You aren't in your computer lab, Wren. Sighing, she set her tablet down on the central table, her gaze on the crystal formation in the center of it.

It wasn't just amazing, it was pretty, too.

Her scans confirmed that the energy the crystals were giving off wasn't dangerous. It was safe for her to be in there.

With her tablet still running scans, Wren dropped down on her butt. Tiredness was dragging on her. She leaned her head back against the wall and sighed. She was so tired. She hadn't slept in a real bed for almost a week. She rubbed her eyes.

Hmm, she knew Malax's bed would be comfy. Even comfier with the war commander in it. *Oh, God.* She rolled her eyes. Their little moment in his cabin aside, she couldn't let herself obsess over the man. One, he wanted to kill her. Two, she'd hijacked his ship. Three...she couldn't think of a three, but she was sure there was another good reason.

Right, focus on your mission. She opened her back-pack and pulled out one of her last energy bars. They tasted one step up from cardboard, but hijackers couldn't be fussy. She munched in silence, enjoying the play of blue light from the crystals.

Without realizing it, Wren dozed off. Her tired brain daydreamed, and she imagined strong arms wrapped around her, a hard body pressed against hers. *"You're safe, Wren. I'll take care of you."*

It had been forever since she'd felt safe. Her space marine father had died when she was little and her mother had turned to alcohol to cope. Her sisters had been her only security. They'd been the ones to pack her lunch and braid her hair.

"You're so beautiful, Wren."

The echo of the deep, dream voice jolted Wren awake. Hmm, interestingly enough, that voice sounded suspiciously like a certain war commander.

Her foot had gone to sleep, and she stretched her leg out, jiggling it to get rid of the uncomfortable pins and needles. She rubbed her eyes and glanced towards her tablet.

She froze.

Her tablet was exactly where she'd left it. But a small, blue crystal was *crawling* on it.

What the hell? She rubbed her eyes again, then rose.

Yep, a small, blue crystal was moving over her tablet screen. As she watched, it began to melt, like it was being absorbed into her tablet.

"No!" She leaped forward and snatched up the tablet. She couldn't afford to lose it. It was the only thing that allowed her access to the ship's systems.

The blue had spread over the screen. She touched it, and it stuck to her fingers like glue. She pulled her hand away, and the substance stretched like bubblegum.

Oh, no. Some was stuck to her hand and she shook her fingers. Then, the blue stuff began to crawl *up* her hand. *Ew.* She shook it again, but the substance wouldn't budge. She watched it circle around her wrist, forming a thin, blue line. She was wearing a small leather bracelet that Eve had given her years ago, and as she watched, the blue goo mimicked the weave of the leather bracelet. She now had a new blue bracelet.

She tugged at it, but it wouldn't budge. *Great.*

Suddenly, her tablet went crazy, the screen blinking and flickering.

"No!" *Not her baby.*

Wren frantically tapped the screen. The blue substance was gone now, except for a faint blue glow around the screen. She tried to reboot the tablet, but the screen stayed stubbornly black.

Come on. Come on. She shook the device. This couldn't be happening to her. Her throat tightened, and she tapped the screen again.

She dropped down, her throat tight and tears threatening. She swallowed, fighting back the burn. She wouldn't cry. As a little girl, she tried not to cry and make things harder for Eve and Lara. Even when she'd found her mom drunk again, or the kids at school had teased her for being smart or a klutz.

All of a sudden, the screen flared to life. She gasped, and her heart started beating again. She tapped in some commands, checking all her data and programs.

She blew out a relieved breath. They were all still there.

"Hello, Wren."

The warm, female voice coming from her tablet almost made her drop it. "Um..."

"I like your Earth technology."

Wren tilted her head. Her tablet hadn't made a communication link with anyone. Who the hell was talking to her?

Feeling more than a little silly, Wren stared at her tablet. "Who are you?"

"I am an Eon helian-enhanced tech crystal. I help run the *Rengard* warship."

Holy cow. "So, you're a program? Or are you alive?"

"I'm both."

Hmm, so this was some sort of Eon, organic-enhanced artificial intelligence. Somehow, the helian had tapped into her tablet.

"Um, so you're just checking out my tablet?"

"I am now bonded with your tablet."

Wren froze. *Oh, shit.* "So, you can un-bond with my tablet?"

"No." The voice sounded amused.

Wren lifted her hand and touched the blue circle around her wrist. "And this?"

"And I've also bonded with you, Wren Traynor." The voice sounded pleased with itself. "I can use the wrist-band to communicate with you."

With her other hand, Wren plucked at the blue band again. It was stuck fast. "I'm not really sure how I feel about this."

Suddenly, the ship shuddered, knocking Wren over. She tumbled to her knees, and then was jerked sideways. She landed on her ass.

"What's happening?" she cried.

"A Kantos kill squad has boarded the *Rengard*," the voice from her tablet said calmly.

"What?" Wren yelped. The damn woman, thing, helian, tablet—whatever the hell the thing was—didn't have to sound so calm about it.

Okay, what now, Wren?

ALARMS WERE SOUNDING all over the bridge.

"Sabin?" Malax barked.

"A Kantos kill squad cut through the hull and boarded near the engine room," his security commander bit out.

Cren-cursed Kantos. "Why didn't we see them coming?"

Sabin's purple-threaded eyes flashed. "Thanks to our Terran hijacker, we didn't have full scanners."

Cren. "Get your security team ready. We'll intercept them."

Malax's security commander nodded and turned to gather his best warriors.

Malax commanded his symbiont, and a second later, black scales burst from his wristband. They flowed up his arm, and then down his body and across his chest, all the way down to encase his legs. Gold glinted in places, and he formed a sword on his arm. It glowed with a golden light.

Grimly, he strode into the corridor, Sabin and his warriors falling in behind him.

"Where are the Kantos headed?" Malax asked.

Sabin looked at the small comp screen attached to his wrist. "The center of the ship. They're moving fast."

Why the cren would they be—? Malax bit off a curse. *No.* There was no way they could know about the *Rengard's* experimental technology. It was a highly protected secret.

But there was no other explanation for where the Kantos were heading, like a missile with a targeting lock.

He drew in a breath. "They're heading for the ship's helian core."

Sabin's jaw firmed. "They can't know."

"They know."

Malax picked up speed. The Kantos were desperate to

get their hands on any helians and any advanced Eon tech. He'd read the reports from War Commander Thann-Eon that he'd seen Kantos weapons with helian signatures. They'd also stolen sacred Eon gems before Lara Traynor and her warrior, Caze Vann-Jad, had retrieved them.

Malax's gut tightened. Eon warriors were bonded with helians very young, as part of their warrior training. It was a difficult transition and a sacred bond of trust. The Eon protected the helians, gave them a chance to use their unique abilities, and in return, they aided the Eon warriors in battle.

What the Kantos did to the helian with their twisted experimentation was a perversion.

Somehow, the Kantos had gotten wind of the *Rengard's* helian-enhanced systems. It was the only warship in the Eon fleet with the technology.

"They're in the large maintenance conduits on Deck Alpha-Five," Sabin said.

The team of warriors charged down another corridor and approached an entrance to the maintenance conduits. These were large enough for them to fit into, but the tunnels still weren't spacious. As he pushed inside, Malax's shoulders brushed the walls. He led his team into the conduit, their boots hammering on the metal floor.

Malax wondered where Wren was. He hoped she was well out of the way, and nowhere near the Kantos.

"They've moved up a level," Sabin said. "And out of the conduits."

Frowning, Malax moved toward a ladder. He climbed quickly, and shoved open the hatch above him.

When they reached the next level, he straightened, then shouldered out a door and into the corridor.

At the end of the hall, he spotted the Kantos kill squad.

Each insectoid soldier had four long, jointed legs, two razor-sharp arms, and a torso covered in armored plates. Their flat faces had four beady, glowing, yellow eyes, and a small mouth filled with sharp teeth.

There were six of them in this squad, and the aliens spread into a line, lifting their arms. He knew the edges of their arms were as sharp as swords. Malax raised his sword as well, the blade glowing gold.

A buzzing noise filled the hall, and he knew that the aliens were communicating with each other.

Malax took several steps, then burst into a run. He heard his team following him.

The Kantos rushed to meet them, flowing on their four legs.

With a grunt, Malax swung his sword. The lead Kantos dodged, but Malax was ready. He'd trained his entire life with his helian-based weapon. And he loved fighting. He loved the thrill of pushing his body, of matching wits with an opponent.

He sidestepped, and lunged in again. The Kantos were his enemy and he wanted them neutralized.

The Kantos soldier was fast, but Malax was faster. He sliced through one of the Kantos' arms. The alien skittered back, blood spraying. Malax leaped up, swung his sword down, and punctured the Kantos' bony chest.

The soldier tilted wildly, knocking into another Kantos.

Malax landed and spun, raising his sword. He glanced around and saw Sabin and the other warriors, fighting hard. Another Kantos soldier broke free of the fight and rushed at Malax. This one was the elite, the leader of this little band. Malax ducked, then surged up with his sword, power sluicing through his body.

He pinned the elite to the wall.

"You never should have boarded my ship," Malax ground out.

We will take all you value.

Cren, he hated when the Kantos spoke telepathically. He yanked his sword back, and the elite slid to the floor.

Then he heard Sabin curse.

"There is another kill squad incoming. They have reinforcements!"

By Ston's sword. Malax's gut churned. Without the ship's systems, they had no way to know how many Kantos were aboard.

The new kill squad rounded the corner, moving as one unit, their yellow-gold eyes glowing.

Malax threw his arms out and charged. He lifted his sword like a lance.

As he neared the aliens, he jumped, skewering the closest Kantos. He let the battle haze wash over him. He didn't think, he merely felt the fight, his body shifting into each move it knew so well.

His warriors joined him. He heard the grunts of his warriors and that low-level, buzzing hum of Kantos communicating with each other.

He watched one of his warriors fall, skewered by a sharp Kantos arm. Blood flowed down the warrior's chest. The Kantos soldier moved to finish the downed warrior.

No. Grim faced, Malax shoved his way toward them. For a second, he was back on Dalath Prime, in his first command position, with his team under ambush and dying all around him.

He collided with the Kantos, knocking the alien away. With several slashes of his sword, he destroyed the soldier.

Malax rushed back to the warrior. He quickly slid his hands under the man's arms, and dragged him away from the main fight. He could see the man's helian was already slowing the blood flow to the wound.

Turning, he watched another warrior get hit. The man's big body flew backward, blood spraying.

By Alqin's axe, they needed reinforcements.

He pressed his communicator. "Bridge, send a second security team, now! Bridge?"

There was no reply.

More humming filled the corridor, and he guessed that the Kantos were jamming the signals. *Cren.* Two more Kantos rushed at him.

He slashed out, and cut off the leg of one Kantos. He turned, dodging out of the way as the other soldier's arm sliced over his head.

Suddenly, the *Rengard* shook. Malax spread his feet to keep his balance.

The Kantos ship had to be firing on them.

"WC, look out!"

Wren's voice made him spin and drop to the floor. From behind him, a Kantos bug leaped over his head.

The dog-sized creature glimmered green, and was covered in sharp spikes. Its sharp mandibles snapped together with tremendous force, right where his head had been.

It landed, and before it could launch another attack, Malax exploded into action with a roar.

He swiped out, cutting into the bug's hard body. It screeched, but he kept pushing on the sword. The tip pierced the shell and slid into the creature.

With another deafening screech, it collapsed.

Panting, Malax rose and scanned the corridor. Where was Wren? Farther down the corridor, he saw a loose panel into the maintenance conduits and Wren peering out, tablet clutched in her hands. He angrily waved her back.

Another Kantos rushed him and he swung his sword. He slashed at the alien, throwing all his power behind the blows. The soldier collapsed.

"Sir, three Kantos broke off," Sabin reported.

Malax spun and heaved in a breath. "Where are they?"

"They moved into the maintenance conduits."

Malax turned, and spotted the ruined panels where the Kantos had entered the conduits. Right where Wren had been hiding.

"Cren!"

"Malax?" Sabin sounded hesitant.

"They're chasing the Terran woman." Malax scowled. "Let's move."

CHAPTER FIVE

The *Rengard* rocked again.

Wren slammed into the side of the tunnel, muttered a curse, and kept crawling. She'd managed to avoid the Kantos chasing her. Thank God she was smaller than they were.

She reached the helian crystal room and clambered inside.

Phew.

Again, the *Rengard* shuddered.

"A Kantos battlecruiser is firing on us," her tablet said.

"Yeah, I got that." Wren shoved her hair out of her eyes. Dammit, she had to find a way to help. This was her fault. If she hadn't hijacked the *Rengard's* systems, the Kantos would never have gotten aboard.

When she'd seen that bug aiming for Malax, and the wounded warriors...

Shaking off the guilt, she lifted her tablet, tapping on

the screen. "Okay, now... Hmm, it would be much easier if you had a name."

"I'd like one," her helian-enhanced tablet responded.

"We'll come up with something. Can you reboot the *Rengard's* systems and give full control back to the bridge?"

"Of course. Initializing." A pause. "Do you really think those big, testosterone-filled warriors are the right people to be running the ship?"

Wren almost snorted. "Yes. It's their ship."

A sniff. "But I believe we could do a better job."

"You're a sassy thing," Wren said.

"Hmm. Sassy. I like that." The intelligence sounded pleased.

Wren shook her head. "I can't wait for you to meet my sisters."

"I like sassy. I believe that should be my name."

"What?" Wren frowned. "No, I... Oh, screw it, why the hell not. Okay, Sassy, let's do a hot reboot."

Data scrolled across the screen, and Wren's fingers flew as she tried to keep up with Sassy. They found a rhythm and soon, Sassy was almost guessing what Wren needed before Wren asked.

Having her own helian AI really helped speed things up.

"There!" Wren cried. She watched as the warship's full systems came online. "Sassy, I need to talk to the bridge crew."

"Line open. Hello, bridge, please listen to my human."

Wren shook her head. "Systems are yours, warriors. Your weapons are online."

"Thank you," a cautious female voice said. In the background, Wren heard a jumble of voices as the warriors leaped into action.

"Where's Malax?" Wren asked. He should have finished with the Kantos soldiers who'd gotten aboard.

"He's busy chasing down some Kantos who escaped."

Wren's stomach rolled. It had to be the ones who'd chased her. "Sassy, where's the war commander?"

"Traveling through the maintenance conduits one deck below us. He appears to be hunting several Kantos soldiers."

"He's okay?"

"He is bleeding."

"What?" Wren's voice rose.

"It is a minor injury, Wren Traynor."

Wren blew out a breath. "We have to help him. Come on."

She crawled out of the helian room and back into the tunnel. Here she was, crawling again. If she ever had to crawl again after this mission, it would be way too soon.

But first, she had to survive the mission.

"What are the Kantos up to?" she murmured aloud.

"Since they are moving in our direction, I deduce they either want you, which is a low probability, or they want the helian crystals."

Wren gasped. *Shit.* They couldn't let the Kantos get their hands on the helians.

She found a tunnel leading down and started

climbing down the ladder. The sound of fighting reached her ears.

Dropping the last meter, her boots hit the floor, and she quickly assessed the scene in front of her. Ahead in the corridor, Malax and three warriors were fighting with several Kantos.

Ugh. The Kantos were ugly.

She switched her gaze from the insectoids to Malax. He leaped into the air, his gold, glowing sword spinning. Her jaw dropped open. Wow, the man could fight. She watched, mesmerized, as he slashed one Kantos and kicked another.

He was power and a brutal, unforgiving force.

She watched him slice that sword so fast it was beginning to blur. He followed through with a punch. As the Kantos soldier slammed into the wall, the metal dented under the impact. A shower of sparks rained out.

"Okay, Sassy, we have to help them."

"I'm ready."

Wren lifted her tablet and swiped the screen. "Good. Okay, let's see what we can do."

"Perhaps an electrical surge?" Sassy suggested.

"I like it. Okay, we need to get the Kantos together and away from the warriors."

She scanned the corridor. Between her and the fight, she spied an air vent.

She tapped in a command. "Sassy, I need you to evacuate that air vent closest to the Kantos."

"Excellent idea, Wren Traynor."

Wren grabbed the wall and a second later, there was a huge rush of sound. The Kantos buzzing increased and the aliens were sucked down the corridor, away from the warriors. The warriors grabbed onto each other, fighting against the pull of air.

Smiling, Wren gripped tight to stop herself being sucked in as well. She forced back the urge to do a fist pump.

Suddenly, Malax's head whipped around and their gazes locked. She saw his mouth moving, but over the noise, she couldn't hear him.

"Surge now, Sassy," she ordered.

"You are too close to the surge radius," Sassy said.

Shit. Before Wren could move, one of the Kantos lifted something in its clawed hand. It looked like a small egg, or pod, or something. The soldier tossed the pod toward the warriors.

Wren watched it arch through the air and burst open. A green poison splattered out, hitting the closest warrior. The man shouted in pain.

Oh, no. She saw the other Kantos pulling out more pods.

"Electrical surge now, Sassy!" Wren yelled.

Electricity exploded from the panel in the wall behind the Kantos. The blue surge ran over the Kantos, and their buzzing turned high-pitched and frantic.

Then pain crashed into Wren.

Oh, ow, ow, ow. She dropped to her knees and saw electricity skating up her arms.

Then the electricity was gone and she collapsed. Her cheek hit the metal grate floor, but all she felt was the agony tearing through her body.

She couldn't breathe or move.

She thought she heard a deep voice shouting her name.

Oh, being a badass really hurt.

MALAX WATCHED Wren crash to the ground.

No.

"Finish the Kantos," he yelled at Sabin. Then he charged toward Wren, his gut clenched tight.

"Malax!" Sabin yelled.

He spun, just as a Kantos bug leaped out of a vent from above.

He caught the creature, twisted his hands, and, using his helian-enhanced strength, cracked its neck. He tossed it aside, then strode to Wren.

The *Rengard* shuddered and he realized his ship was firing. Airen clearly had control of the ship's weapons again.

Bending one knee, he dropped down beside Wren. She was lying on her belly and so still. He realized now that in his cabin earlier, she'd never been motionless. Not once. She'd vibrated with energy.

Gently, he rolled her over. The side of her face was covered with terrible burns. A muscle in his jaw jumped.

He lifted her into his arms. She barely weighed a thing.

"Call the infirmary. Send Thane to my cabin."

His security commander gave him a look, then Sabin's gaze dropped to Wren. The man nodded.

Malax jogged through the corridors, heading to his

cabin. He could hear her heartbeat, so he knew she was still alive, but it was weak.

The panic trickling inside him was so unfamiliar that he wasn't sure how to deal with it.

He burst into his cabin and gently laid her on his bed. He pressed his palm to her chest and felt it rising and falling jerkily.

A moment later, his door chimed and his medical commander entered.

The *Rengard's* doctor was several years older than Malax, and wore his hair shorter than most warriors. Thane Kann-Eon's body was tall and powerful, even as silver dusted his temples. He was one of the best doctors in the Eon fleet. The unmated doctor was dedicated to his work.

"Heal her," Malax demanded.

The doctor nodded, dropping down on the edge of the bed. He lifted a scanner and pressed his fingers to Wren's neck.

"She has unique physiology compared to the Eon—"

"I said heal her, Thane, not study her."

The doctor nodded again and got to work.

"She's going to be okay?" Malax asked.

"She will, if you don't continue to interrupt me."

Malax figured that if his medical commander was annoyed, Wren would be fine. Still, Malax stood by the bed, arms crossed, watching everything the doctor did. Wren's dark curls were spread out over his pillow, her cheeks pale. He had to fight not to touch her.

The door chimed again, and Airen appeared. Malax looked back at Wren. "The Kantos?"

"We now have full control of the ship's systems, so we fired on the Kantos cruiser. They retreated. I have several teams doing sweeps for any remaining bugs or soldiers, but now that the scanners are working, we aren't detecting any Kantos signatures."

He met Airen's gaze. "Full control?"

His second's gaze flicked to Wren and back. "She contacted me and returned control once the Kantos boarded."

His gaze moved over Wren's face and he frowned. Confounding little Terran.

"Now that the systems are functional, we have incoming messages from the Eon High Command, and from War Commander Thann-Eon and Ambassador Thann-Eon from the *Desteron*. They are demanding to talk to you."

"Take the calls for me."

"Me?" The woman's eyebrows rose.

"Tell them I'll contact them as soon as I can."

Airen looked at him, speechless for a second. It was rare for Malax to ignore a call from Eon High Command. He ignored her and strode to the bed. He dropped down and picked up Wren's hand. It was limp in his.

He watched Thane press an injector to her neck and administer a stim. Next, the doctor held up a small vial. The havv glowed red inside the glass. The bio-organisms, similar to the helians, had been created by one of the first Eon warriors, Eschar. Thane dripped some of the thick, red fluid onto Wren's face. It flowed over her burns and the red glow intensified as the healing began.

Finally, Thane stepped back. "She's going to be fine."

Malax let out a shuddering breath and nodded.

His doctor looked amused. "Maybe I should sedate you, instead of her?"

He shot his medical commander an arch look.

Suddenly, Wren's eyelids fluttered open. She looked at him and shot him a lazy smile, then she glanced at Thane.

"Ooh, a silver fox." She made a humming noise and her eyes closed again. "Nice dream."

Malax cleared his throat. "Wren—"

"Hmm? I'm having an awesome dream. Instead of one hunky man at my bedside, there are two."

Malax shook his head. "I see you're feeling better."

Her blue eyes popped open. "Save the moody for later, WC, you're ruining my dream."

He gently squeezed her hand. "You should never have come near the fight with the Kantos, Wren."

She sighed and squeezed her eyes closed. "I'm not dreaming, am I?"

"No."

"The Kantos?"

"Gone."

Her eyes opened fully, and she propped herself higher on the pillows. She glanced at the doctor. "Hi, I'm Wren Traynor from Earth."

The warrior's lips twitched. "Medical Commander Thane Kann-Eon."

"You work for War Commander Grumpy?"

Thane made a strangled sound. "Yes."

Malax rolled his eyes to the ceiling and growled.

"You don't like that one?" she said. "How about War Commander Bossy?"

"Thank you for returning control of my ship," Malax said.

She waved a hand. "Oh, it was nothing. My choices were death by Kantos kill squad, or destruction of Earth and sacrificing my sisters. Easy choice." The humor dissolved from her face, and he saw sadness move through her eyes.

"Your sisters?" The doctor frowned. "I thought they were safe aboard the *Desteron*?"

Wren went still and looked into Malax's eyes, then she glanced at the doctor again.

"Wren doesn't believe me," Malax said.

"War commanders never lie," Thane said.

"You must be hungry," Malax said.

Her eyes lit. "I've been starving for days. Space Corps rations leave a lot to be desired."

Malax moved to his synthesizer and keyed in some Eon dishes he thought would suit her Terran physiology. When he brought the plate back, she eyed it hungrily.

Thane nodded. "Good choices. They'll provide her with the nutrition she needs."

Wren grabbed some things, taking huge bites. She moaned. "I have no idea what this is, but it's great." She shoved some more in her mouth.

Malax bit back a smile, enjoying watching her pleasure at eating. Many women in his acquaintance ate delicately, but not Wren. She ate with an enthusiasm he liked.

She tried some other delicacies and moaned again.

Malax found his gaze drifting to her lips, watching as she licked them.

"This almost tastes like cheese." She paused. "Now I have a huge craving for a hot dog topped with cheese, ketchup, and mustard."

He had no idea what any of those things were. "I'm sure if you give my chef the right information, he can replicate a hot dog for you."

She chewed and swallowed. "That would be awesome." She licked her fingers.

Malax's communicator beeped and he heard one of his communications team. "War Commander, we've made contact with the *Desteron*."

He touched his communicator. "I'll take the call in my cabin." He looked at Wren. "Would you like to talk to your sisters?"

Wren's eyes lit up, even though there was still skepticism on her face. "Yes. Thank you."

"You can thank me by ensuring that you do *not* electrocute yourself again. Or go near any fights with the Kantos."

"Sure thing." She shot him a smile that Malax didn't trust for a second.

CHAPTER SIX

Wren lay on the bed, grateful that whatever the doc had given her was making the last of her pain fade away.

The doctor had left and as Malax rose to get a comp screen, she sat up, and touched her face. There was little sign of any injury, just smooth, tender skin. Man, Eon tech was awesome.

She took in Malax's broad back, then smoothed a hand over her hair. Ugh, it was a tangled mess.

He returned, sitting on the bed beside her, making it dip. He held up the sleek tablet and the screen flickered. A man's face appeared. He was a typical, rugged Eon warrior, with a hard glint in his blue-black eyes. He looked like a man used to being in charge.

"War Commander Thann-Eon," Malax said.

"War Commander Dann-Jad. I'm pleased to hear that your ship is back under your control."

"As am I."

"And your...cargo?"

"Safe," Malax answered.

Cargo? Wren frowned. What were they talking about?

"And your hijacker?" Thann-Eon continued.

"Is fine. We had a small run-in with the Kantos, but she's recovered from her injuries."

Malax tilted the screen so Wren could see it better. She eyed the imposing man looking back at her.

He wore the exact same uniform as Malax, and his hair was a shade darker. Somehow, War Commander Thann-Eon looked more intimidating.

"He looks intense," she whispered to Malax.

"He can hear you," Malax responded.

Thann-Eon smiled, the expression transforming his face into something quite handsome. "You must be Wren."

"I'm told my sisters are aboard your ship." Wren couldn't keep the disbelief out of her voice. "And I was also told a bunch of other crazy things—"

"They're probably true," the war commander interrupted her. "War commanders never—"

"—lie." She wrinkled her nose. "So I've heard."

"Is that her?" A female voice broke through. "Why didn't you wait for me?"

A woman shoved her way in front of the war commander.

Wren leaned forward, unconsciously gripping Malax's arm. "Eve?"

"Wren!" Eve cried.

There was another muffled voice, and a second woman pushed in beside Eve.

"Oh, God." Wren's fingers tightened further on Malax. "Lara!"

"Are you okay?" Lara, always the big sister, demanded. "Are those freshly healed wounds on your face?"

"We had a slight altercation with the Kantos." Wren waved a hand. "I helped save my war commander's ass."

Eve rose a dark brow. "*Your* war commander?"

Wren's cheeks heated and she knew she was blushing. She released Malax's arm. "Well, not *mine*, per se." What worked best with her sisters was a swift distraction. "I've been told some rather crazy things about you two."

Eve smiled up at Thann-Eon and Wren's chest hitched. *Oh, God.* Her sister looked radiant.

Lara nodded, smiling. "All true. The war commander here belongs to Eve, and my warrior is the *Desteron's* security commander."

Wren shook her head. "How is this even possible? You two, mated?"

Eve tucked a strand of her hair behind her ear. "Well, it all started when I kidnapped Davion and we crash-landed on a hunter planet."

"And it continued when Space Corps blackmailed me into stealing sacred Eon gems, and the Eon sent Caze to hunt me down," Lara continued.

"Fucking Space Corps," the three sisters all said at once.

Wren smiled at them, emotion burning in her chest. Despite the odds, they'd survived. She listened, rapt, as her sisters recapped their adventures. Several times, Wren gasped or cursed. She couldn't stop herself from squeezing Malax's brawny arm again. Between kidnappings, starship crashes, wild fights with the Kantos, and passionate matings with Eon warriors, it was a lot to take in.

"What happens now?" Wren asked, feeling more than slightly overwhelmed.

"War Commander Dann-Jad, I ask that you rendezvous with the *Desteron* so my sister can come aboard," Eve said.

At the mention of her leaving the *Rengard*, a funny feeling flared in Wren's chest. Her gaze clashed with Malax's.

"Right," Wren said weakly. "Sounds like a plan."

Eve nodded. "We could use your skills in the fight against the Kantos, Wren. They aren't going away any time soon."

Wren nodded. "Okay."

All of a sudden, the screen started to flicker and the sound distorted.

"Eve? Lara?"

Malax leaned closer, his arm brushing hers and making her pulse jump. He frowned at the screen.

"Airen?" He touched his communicator. "What's wrong with the communication?"

"We have a problem," Airen said.

"What now?"

"It looks like the Kantos planted a bug swarm somewhere on the ship while they were aboard. Something is destroying parts of our system components."

Malax pinched the bridge of his nose and muttered something Wren suspected was a curse.

"Where?" he asked.

"We can't track them," Airen answered. "Systems are going down all over the place, making it impossible to get a fix."

"Find the swarm, Airen. Get teams out there searching."

"Yes, sir."

Malax shoved a hand through his hair, looking irate.

"This is my fault," Wren said.

"No, it's the Kantos who are to blame."

"But they wouldn't have been aboard if I hadn't hijacked—"

He reached out and cupped her face. The feel of those callused fingers on her skin made her chest tighten. It made it hard to breathe.

Don't, Wren. The last thing she needed was an inappropriate attraction to this man. She'd sworn off men. She pulled her face away from his touch.

"We'll find these bugs," he said.

"I may be able to help," a female voice said.

Malax looked startled. He scanned the room. Wren looked over and spotted her tablet resting beside the bed.

"Um..." Wren mumbled.

His brow creased. "Who just spoke?"

"Me," Sassy replied.

His gold-black gaze zeroed in on her tablet. For a second, the gold strands in his eyes seemed to glow.

Wren cleared her throat. "War Commander Dann-Jad, meet Sassy."

"Sassy?" he asked cautiously.

"My tablet."

"Your tablet talks?"

"Well, it never used to, but it does now."

"I enjoy talking," Sassy added unhelpfully.

Malax crossed his arms over his chest. "Explain, woman."

Oh, he was going all warrior on her. "Weeeell, it's now my tablet-slash-helian-enhanced intelligence."

His arms dropped to his sides. "What?" he breathed.

"It's kind of a long story."

"I am one of the *Rengard's* helians from the central helian core. Wren paid a visit to the core and I was curious about her tech. The merge was unintentional...mostly."

Malax hissed out a breath. "*Cren.*"

"I absorbed Wren's Terran tech, bonded with Wren, and I've now evolved," Sassy said.

Wren held up her wrist and the blue band glowed. She smiled weakly. "Surprise."

MALAX WALKED onto the bridge with Wren at his side.

She was studying her surroundings, curiosity in her eyes and her hair a tumble of curls around her face.

He strode over to the light table where Airen was standing. His second eyed Wren for a moment, then nodded at him. Nearby, Sabin stood quietly, watching Wren like she might attack them at any second.

"Airen and Sabin, I'd like to introduce Wren Traynor. Wren, these are my two top warriors. Second Commander Airen Kann-Felis and Security Commander Sabin Solann-Ath."

Wren waved. "Hi. Sorry about the whole hijacking thing."

His warriors both nodded cautiously.

"Scans?" Malax asked.

Airen swiped the table. "As you can see, we've marked the areas of damage, but we can't locate the bugs."

Malax stared at the detailed schematic of the *Rengard* and the areas marked in red. Wren leaned over as well.

"Ooh, I love this comp table." She stroked the edge of it.

Her trousers stretched over her curves and his gaze dropped. A body like that should be outlawed. She was so different from the tall, toned Eon women. He felt his own body responding and he fought for some control. When he looked up, he saw several of his warriors also staring at her.

He glared at them, and that was all it took for them to snap back to attention at their consoles.

Airen set her hands on her hips. "It looks like it's a small swarm of some kind of bug we haven't seen before."

An image appeared on the screen, obviously taken from a camera somewhere in the ship. It showed a cloud of small, black bugs zooming down a corridor.

"They've chewed through some components on decks Beta-Three and Delta-One." Airen shook her head.

"We have to find them. Soon. Before they damage a critical system."

"I might be able to help." Wren set her tablet onto the light table.

Airen frowned at her. "I don't think—"

Malax held up his hand. "If you think you can help, we'd appreciate it." He stared at the tablet. "And then I'll need my team to analyze your tablet afterward."

"Analyze her tablet?" Airen's brows rose. "It looks like inferior Terran technology to me—"

"I am not inferior," came Sassy's voice. "I'm *very* advanced."

Airen blinked.

"There's a helian in there," Malax said.

His second's mouth dropped open. "What?"

"Hel-lo," Wren said. "We have Kantos bugs to find. You can worry about Sassy later."

Airen just looked confused now. "Sassy?"

"That's her name." Wren swiped at the tablet screen. "Okay, Sassy, tap into the *Rengard*'s main systems."

"Doing it now," Sassy responded.

Sabin stiffened and took a step forward. "War Commander, that's a security risk."

Malax held his hand up again. "It's fine. Wren has no plans to hijack the ship again." He shot her a look.

She screwed up her nose. "No."

"And technically," he continued, ignoring her, "Sassy is part of the *Rengard*. She's just absorbed Wren's tech."

"Sassy, I have an algorithm you could use that takes the bugs' last locations and areas of damage, then it'll run some probabilities," Wren said.

"On it." A pause. "Hmm, those little bugs are playing hard to get," Sassy said. "Ah, there they are."

Wren nodded, swiping the screen. "Sassy's found them. She's narrowed it down to deck Gamma-Two."

"Redirect the search teams," Malax ordered.

Sabin straightened. "I'll join the lead team." The tall man swiveled and strode off the bridge.

"It's still a large area to search," Airen said.

"I know." Wren kept tapping, her fingers moving like lightning. "Sassy, I have a program we can try—"

She kept speaking to her tablet, Sassy responding. Malax watched Wren work, completely absorbed and working with quick intelligence. Her eyes were alive, and he suspected she had fully forgotten she was on the bridge of an Eon warship.

The woman was mesmerizing.

She lifted her head and smiled at him.

He scowled back at her, wondering how she could have this effect on him. Her smile faltered.

"Um, I've narrowed it down. The bugs are definitely in this section of that deck." She tapped the schematic of the *Rengard* on the light table, circling the location.

Malax nodded. "Good work, Wren." He glanced at Airen. His second touched her earpiece, sending orders to redirect the search teams.

"There's something else," Wren added.

"Yes?"

"These bugs are getting awfully close to your ship's main stabilizers."

Malax felt his muscles tighten. The stabilizers maintained the ship's orientation. And right beside the stabilizers was the gravity system.

"Team One is going in," Airen said.

A screen on the wall flickered and footage appeared. They turned to watch. The feed was coming from a camera on Sabin's armor. The security commander was now decked out in his black-scale armor, along with his security team. The search team all had their helian armor on, moving in tight formation through a maintenance conduit.

Suddenly, shouts broke out. A black swarm engulfed the warriors.

Wren gasped. "Oh, God."

They stood, frozen in shock. Malax ground his teeth together. The shouts of his warriors echoed in his ears.

"They're going in through a crack," someone shouted.

"Someone stop them!"

"Bring the flamethrowers," Sabin yelled.

Suddenly, the *Rengard* began to tilt to the left. Malax gripped the edge of the light table to stay upright.

"The bugs have damaged the stabilizers," Sassy said calmly.

Around the bridge, warriors cursed and clung to their consoles.

Malax saw Wren stagger and reached for her. His hand closed on hers, just as the gravity system failed.

His boots left the floor, and as she started to float upward, Wren gave a startled squeak. He wrapped an arm around her, pulling her into his chest. She clung to him.

"Get the engineers down there," Malax ordered.

"We need to stop those bugs first." Airen was still gripping the light table, her feet floating above her head.

Malax's head brushed the ceiling, and he braced himself, holding Wren tight. "I need ideas, warriors."

Wren tapped her lips. "Hmm."

He glanced down at her, instantly distracted by the full, plump shape of her mouth. *Cren.* He had a disabled ship to worry about, not Wren Traynor's delectable mouth.

"I have an idea," she said. "Sassy, are these bugs attracted to sound?"

"I believe so, yes." Sassy's voice came from the floating tablet.

"I have a few Kantos bug noises stored in my data," Wren said. "Can you generate a noise at the right frequency to attract them?"

"Yes."

Wren swiveled to look up at Malax. "You need to get me close to the bugs. Sassy can generate the sound, and you need to find something to trap them in."

He pulled her closer. "I can organize that."

"So, we have a plan."

He nodded. "Hold on."

He pressed a boot to the wall and pushed off. Wren snatched her tablet from mid-air as they floated past.

"Airen, I need containment boxes brought down to deck Gamma-Two."

"I'll arrange it."

Malax zoomed out of the doors of the bridge, keeping Wren flush against his body. They flew down the corridor.

"Ooh, I always wanted to fly," Wren said.

He shook his head. Nothing seemed to faze this woman. She'd been sent to hijack a high-tech, alien warship and hadn't hesitated. Now, she was going to capture Kantos bugs without any gravity, and she sounded excited. Whatever situation crept up, she appeared to simply adjust her strategy and charge onward.

He tightened his hold on her and found his nose buried in her hair. He pulled in a deep breath of her scent, something warm beneath the lingering traces of his soap.

Focus, Dann-Jad. After they contained the Kantos bugs, then he'd deliver Wren to the *Desteron*. He'd probably never see her again. She was a confounding little Terran, and definitely not for him.

He only had room in his life for his ship and his warriors.

CHAPTER SEVEN

Malax expertly maneuvered them through the corridors and down a malfunctioning lift shaft. He moved with ease and didn't bump them into anything once. Wren was a little in awe. She'd have donked her head half a dozen times by now.

She was actually digging having no gravity. It was fun.

Especially when you were pressed up against a hard, male body.

She knew she shouldn't be focused on Malax's muscles, but she felt so small tucked up against him. He made her feel safe, protected. Even Lance had never made her feel like that. She knew that whatever they faced, Malax Dann-Jad would face it head on.

They moved into another corridor, and she heard the faint buzzing of the Kantos insects.

Holding Malax with one hand, she pulled out her tablet with the other. She tapped the screen and saw

Sassy was finished generating a sound that should attract the bugs.

She pressed her lips together. *Hopefully*.

As she concentrated, her body drifted from Malax's. He pulled her closer, one big hand gripping her hip to hold her in place.

It was terribly distracting. *Focus, Wren. And not on the strong fingers digging into your skin.* Or on what else he could do with those fingers.

Besides, she was headed for the *Desteron* and her sisters soon. A warrior like Malax would never be interested in her, and soon she'd never see him again.

On that depressing thought, she looked up. "Okay, this should work...I think."

His eyes narrowed. "You *think*? That's not good enough, Wren."

"Sorry, Mr. War Commander, but I don't have the time or resources to run any tests right now."

He blew out a breath and nodded. "All right." He touched his communicator. "Airen, are the containment boxes ready?"

"Ready, Malax. The team is just around the corner from you, putting them in place."

Malax pushed off the wall again, moving them closer. Wren spotted the long, narrow panel that had to lead into a conduit. Behind it, she heard the humming buzz. Yeah, they were in there.

She heard a clunking noise and looked over her shoulder. Several warriors appeared, shifting some large boxes into position.

The humming increased.

Malax moved them away from the panel, and Wren almost dropped her tablet. She grabbed for it and bumped her knee against the wall. *Ow*. She shifted, and her elbow jabbed Malax in the jaw.

"Sorry. I'm a klutz."

He rubbed her elbow and tucked it back in front of her. "We're ready."

"Okay," she said. "Sassy, we're a go." She touched the screen and the sound started. The discordant buzzing was far louder than the insects. She winced. It wasn't pleasant.

Nearby, she heard the warriors groan and clamp their hands over their ears. Malax made a pained sound.

"Oh, God." She hadn't thought. She knew that the Eon warriors had more acute hearing than humans. "Sassy, lower the volume."

The sound dropped a fraction and she saw Malax's face relax a little.

Then there was a buzz of sound. They turned and she saw the panel burst off the conduit. A rush of black insects poured out of the hole.

They rushed at Malax and Wren.

Ugh. She batted at them. They buzzed around her, covering her with some sort of sticky goo. It felt like honey and smelled terrible.

"It's working," someone yelled.

The swarm rushed over Wren and Malax. She felt more of the sticky substance splatter onto them.

She shifted her arm and her tablet closer to the containment boxes. The bugs flew inside. It was working!

"They're all in," Malax said.

She shut off the sound. The warriors quickly slammed the boxes closed. From within, she could hear a muffled, angry buzzing.

The Kantos bugs were trapped.

Eon warriors were shaking their heads and tugging on their ears, but they were smiling.

"Eww." Wren lifted a hand. It was coated in a pale-green, sticky substance. She tried flinging some of the goo off, but it wasn't budging. "Gross." It looked like snot.

Malax swiped some of the gunk off his face. It was totally unfair he still looked rugged and hot, despite the icky substance.

"The bugs are contained, War Commander," his security commander said.

"Well done, Wren," Malax said. "Excellent work."

She felt a flush of pleasure. "I *am* very good at what I do."

"A-hem." Sassy's voice. "I had something to do with it, too."

"Yeah, yeah," Wren said. "Quit trying to steal my thunder."

A faint smile appeared on Malax's face. "You are definitely not a klutz with your tablet."

Her flush deepened.

Malax turned to his security commander. "Sabin, I want these containment boxes destroyed. Incinerate them."

The man nodded and turned to the warriors. Moments later, they moved off, the boxes floating between them.

"Come on." Malax maneuvered Wren down the

corridor. "We need to clean up. Hopefully, my engineers will have the gravity system back on soon."

"I get another shower?"

He made an amused sound. "Well, once we have gravity again, you can."

Wren closed her eyes and moaned. She'd shower three times a day if she could, to catch up after the last week.

When she opened her eyes, she saw Malax staring at her, a strange, intense look on his face. Her belly flipflopped. His gaze traced her face, falling to her lips.

She felt the arc of attraction between them and it made her chest hitch.

Then he looked away. "Come on."

WITH WREN WRAPPED in his arms, Malax sailed down the corridor toward his cabin. There were several items floating through the hall—some tools, a comp screen, and a pair of boots. He made a note to remind his warriors to secure all items aboard the ship.

"War Commander." Airen's voice came through his communicator. "The engineers haven't quite fixed the gravity systems, but they've patched it enough to return gravity to the main decks. Prepare for gravity reinitialization."

"Acknowledged. Thanks, Airen."

He pulled himself to a stop and gripped an air vent above his head. "Hold on."

Wren wrapped her fingers around the vent and a

second later, he felt the gravity kick in. The floating items dropped like stones, clunking on the metal grate floor.

Malax let go. He dropped to the floor, bending his knees to absorb the impact.

"Oh, God." Wren let out a strangled sound and he saw her falling. Her arms and legs were flailing.

He caught her against his chest, the air rushing out of her.

"Um, thanks."

"Are you okay?"

"Peachy." She sniffed. "Except for this horrid smelling gunk."

He set her on her feet. "You can have a shower now." He nudged her toward his cabin and seconds later, followed her inside. "I need to synthesize some new clothes to fit you." No Eon clothes would come close to fitting her.

"This alien goo is gross." Her nose wrinkled and she rubbed her fingers together.

He walked to the synthesizer and tapped on the screen. "We should have the other damaged components fixed soon, then we can set a course for the *Desteron*."

"I can help," she said.

He turned to look at her. "I would appreciate that."

Their gazes locked and they kept staring at each other.

The synthesizer beeped, and Malax cleared his throat. "The washroom is all yours." He waved a hand.

With a nod, she took the clothes he held out to her. The door slid closed behind her.

Touching his own sticky hair, he winced. He smelled

really bad. He needed a shower and clean clothes of his own. As he gathered the supplies he needed, he heard the shower turn on.

Instantly, he imagined her naked. Those curves, her gleaming skin, and those dark curls. His cock went hard and he swallowed a groan. His hand slid into his pocket and he pulled out the scrap of pink lace.

He should return them. He fingered the delicate fabric, imagining what it would look like on her. Desire was a hot burn inside him and he stared at the door. All his life, Malax had dedicated himself to his career, to pleasing his father, and then to protecting his family and those under his command.

He never took anything for himself. He always put the needs of others before his own. He fingered the lace again. For the first time in his life, he wanted something so badly, it hurt.

Malax blew out a breath. Wren wasn't his. She was Terran and would soon be off his ship.

His fingers closed around the panties. He wasn't giving them back. He quickly exited his cabin and entered the adjoining one, which was vacant, to shower and change. Under the blasts of misty water, he kept imagining Wren. With a groan, he let his hand slide down his body. He needed to do something to relieve himself, or his control might slip and he'd do something he regretted. His fingers curled around his cock.

A short while later, he stepped back into his cabin. Wren was still bathing, and now he heard her singing. Badly.

He shook his head, smiling. What she lacked in talent, she made up for in enthusiasm.

Then he heard her scream.

Every muscle in his body locked tight. He hurried to the door, overriding the electronic lock. He rushed inside.

She was naked in the shower stall and he charged toward her. He snaked an arm around her, searching for the threat.

"What's wrong? What's happened?"

Her cheeks turned pink. "Um...the water went cold."

His brows drew together. "The Kantos aren't in here?"

"No. Sorry."

Malax tried to calm his racing pulse. That was when he realized his hands were touching warm, damp skin. Naked skin.

His gaze dropped, skating over her body. She was pressed against him, turning his uniform damp. Her full breasts were plumped up against his chest, and he saw pretty, pink nipples.

Her blush deepened. "Malax."

He loved hearing her say his name. "Wren."

"Oh, God, I'm naked!"

"I noticed."

She held her hands up to her chest. "Stop noticing."

"That would be impossible. You're beautiful." He grabbed a drying cloth and held it out to her. She quickly wrapped it around her body.

She shoved her wet hair back. "You're probably used to women with sleek, toned muscles. Not round bellies and curvy hips."

He frowned, realizing she was embarrassed. "Yes, Eon woman are generally taller and more muscular."

The drying cloth had stuck to her damp skin in patches, giving him small, peekaboo glimpses of her. For some reason, he found it just as provocative. His unruly body was throbbing now. He'd never felt a loss of control like this. Certainly not with any of his casual bed partners.

Wren gave an awkward laugh. "Well, I'm not muscular. At all."

"You're beautiful, soft, fascinating. I find the differences very intriguing."

She swallowed, eyeing him. "Sure you do."

"Remember, a war commander never lies."

Malax sensed the pulse fluttering in her throat. Then he picked up her scent. This time, it was spiked with her arousal. He swallowed a groan.

"You're all perfect." She waved at his body.

"Perfect depends on the beholder's point of view." Because he couldn't stop himself, he reached out and touched her hair. He ran the damp, silky strands through his fingers.

"I would have thought that warriors liked strong, muscled badasses."

"Quiet," he demanded. "No one can say what I like except me."

She stared up at him.

"There are numerous ways to be a badass, Wren. Like having the courage and skills to hijack a warship. Or evading detection for days. Or helping capture a swarm of dangerous Kantos bugs."

Her chest was rising and falling. "You find me attractive?"

"Immensely. It must be obvious."

Her gaze dropped and when it hit the bulge at the front of his trousers, she sucked in a breath. "Oh." Her gaze flicked back up. "This is probably a bad idea."

"Probably."

"I hijacked your ship, I'm leaving soon..."

"Yes." His hands curled into fists.

"Screw it." Wren moved fast, leaping on him.

She surprised Malax and as he caught her, he almost stumbled. Then he wrapped his arms around her, loving the feel of her against him. He spun and pressed her back to the washroom wall.

Then his mouth was on hers.

He drove his tongue into her mouth and her tongue met his. She moaned, rubbing against him. Her taste. He wanted more. Desire exploded inside him.

"My, God—" she mumbled against his lips "—you can kiss."

"More." The word was barely understandable, coated in possession.

"So you like curvy, geeky, and a bit clumsy?" she gasped.

"I like sweet, sexy, and smart."

She shimmied against him and with a growl, he deepened the kiss. He slid his hand into her hair, tilting her head back. He let his tongue plunge deep.

The drying cloth slipped off her body. He pushed her up, closing his mouth on one of her pretty nipples.

"Oh! Oh, Malax." Her hands gripped his hair.

He looked at her face and saw pure pleasure on it. Her eyes were closed and more color ran along her cheekbones. He took his time, lavishing her breasts with attention. As he sucked on one plump nipple, he couldn't get enough of her. He moved across to the other breast.

"That is so good," she gasped.

He stroked a hand down her body. He urged her legs around his waist, stroking her hip, then he slid one hand between their bodies. His fingers dipped between her legs.

"Yes." She bucked against him.

"You feel so soft."

He stroked the delicate folds. She was damp and soft. He stroked, exploring, watching her face for what she liked. He found the hard nub of her clit and pinched it gently.

"Yes, Malax." She bucked against him. "Don't you dare stop."

"You want more?"

"Yes, please."

And Malax wanted nothing more than to give her pleasure and watch this small Terran come apart for him.

CHAPTER EIGHT

"Y**ou're so soft here."

Malax's words rumbled through Wren. She tightened her legs on him, her hands tugging on his hair. He was stroking her and it felt mind-blowingly amazing.

She rolled her hips, riding his hand. A second later, he slid one thick finger inside her.

She moaned. "Oh, God."

This time he groaned. "So tight. So warm and wet."

He added another finger and she felt the sweet sting as her body stretched to accommodate him.

"Ride my fingers, Wren. Take what you need."

She didn't care about the noises she made. He held her against the wall with ease, stroking her closer to her release.

She felt the giant orgasm building, looming on the horizon. Here she was, riding the fingers of the sexiest man she'd ever seen.

"So sweet." He kept working her. "You like this?"

"Yes, God, yes."

"I can smell you. I can feel your body clamping down on my fingers."

He kept stroking, driving her upward. A second later, her climax hit like a tidal wave.

Wren gave a strangled cry, coming hard. "Malax!"

Waves of pleasure swamped her, and it felt like hours before she finally flopped against him, boneless. She felt *so* good.

His hand pulled away and he kept her pinned to the wall by his hard body. As she watched, he lifted his hand and licked his fingers.

Her belly spasmed.

"Very sweet," he murmured.

Jeez. She was turned on again. She licked her lips. "Malax—"

He nudged his hips forward and a very hard bulge rubbed between her lips. Oh, yes, she wanted that. Now.

Suddenly, his communicator beeped. "War Commander?"

He closed his eyes.

Oh, no. Wren wanted to cry.

He opened his eyes. "Go ahead, Airen."

"Malax, the engineers are having trouble repairing some components in the gravity system. They've requested Wren's help."

Oh, man. Talk about bad timing. Malax looked at her, his gold-black gaze intense. For a second, she lost herself, staring at those golden strands.

"Wren?"

Oh, right. She nodded, resigned.

"She'll help," he said.

"They're on deck Beta-Four, section five," Airen said.

"Tell them to expect her soon."

He thumbed the communicator on his belt and the line closed.

"Um, well..." Wren had been hoping for more. A lot more. She'd wanted to slide that uniform off him and get her hands on all that sexy, bronze skin.

He tucked her hair behind her ear. "Thank you for helping."

God, maybe this was for the best. Things had gotten...way out of hand. "Sure. Um, thanks for the orgasm?"

He smiled. "That was my pleasure. We'll talk later. I'd like you to sit with me at dinner."

She smiled, suddenly breathless. A date with an Eon warrior. With Malax. "I should say no. We both know you and I make no sense."

He leaned down. "I disagree."

"Okay," she breathed.

He ran a finger down her nose, then set her back on her feet. He snatched up the drying cloth and wrapped it around her.

"I need to get to the bridge," he said.

She nodded, watching as he strode to his closet and stripped off his damp shirt. *Oh, man.* All those muscles. He pulled on a dry shirt. *Down, girl.*

He shot her a smile. "I'll see you later, Wren."

"Later." She stared at the closed door for a good while before she gave a little scream and grinned. She knew this was risky, and a bit crazy, and possibly one part stupid, but screw it. Malax Dann-Jad was no douchebag like Lance Palmer.

She pulled on the clothes he'd synthesized for her. They were a smaller version of the Eon uniform the warriors on the ship wore. The trousers were a little long and snug in a few places, but they'd do. She looked over her shoulder. Yep, the trousers cupped her butt like a jealous lover.

"Sassy, I need you to lead me to deck Beta-Four, section five."

Her tablet flared to life. "You got it, Wren."

She finger-combed her hair, tugging it back into a ponytail.

"Before you head off," Sassy said. "There are some messages for the War Commander on his console. They downloaded before the systems malfunctioned."

"So? I'm sure he'll get to them."

"They are personal messages."

Curiosity burned through Wren. It was one of her worst habits. She wanted to know more about Malax.

She saw the comp screen on the desk flicker. "Sassy, don't—"

An image filled the screen and when Wren saw the four gorgeous Eon women, her stomach dropped.

"Hey, Mal!" One of the women yelled, smiling brightly.

"We're missing you and wanted to say hi," the tallest woman said, blowing a kiss.

They were all brunettes, all striking, their sleeveless gowns showing off toned arms. What the hell? Did he keep a damn harem?

"So, how are things in deep space, big brother?" another of the women asked. "Staying safe, I hope."

Wren's shoulders relaxed and she let out a laugh. These were his *sisters*. Looking at them now, she saw that three of them had gold-black eyes like Malax, and while the fourth had black-green eyes, her features were a feminine version of Malax's.

"I hope you're back on Jad soon," the youngest woman said. "I need a new transport and want you to come shopping with me."

"And Narla wants you to help her fix some things at her residence," the tall woman said.

The one with the green-black eyes shot a fiery look at her sister. "I do not."

"You do. It's why you haven't hired someone to do it for you. You expect your brother to do it."

Narla tossed her brown hair over one slim shoulder. "Well, he always does a better job. And he always takes care of us."

Hmm, sounded like Malax's sisters had no qualms asking him for whatever they needed. Ever since she'd finished school, Wren had made a point to try not to burden her sisters. They'd given up so much helping to raise her when their mother lost herself in alcoholism. Who looked after Malax? He had a demanding job and clearly, a loving, but demanding family.

"Okay, we'll go now. Mother says hi." All four women waved and smiled.

Sassy's voice filled the room. "There is another—"

"No more of Malax's private messages."

"I thought you'd be interested. Based on your vitals

83

and hormone levels earlier, I know you and the war commander—"

"Sassy! No monitoring my vitals."

"But you are my human," Sassy said. "I need to ensure your health and wellbeing."

Wren pinched her nose. "Let's just get to deck Beta-Four, Sassy."

"Wren—"

"I said lead the way." She didn't have time to discuss the intricacies of her love life with her helian-enhanced tablet right now. "We have work to do."

MALAX SAT BEHIND HIS DESK, listening to the status reports from Airen and Sabin.

But his mind was still focused on Wren.

By Ston's sword, he wished they could have finished what they'd started in his washroom. He wanted her in his bed, that sweet body naked, her whimpers echoing in his ears. Need was a constant gnaw in his gut.

He could still smell her, feel her skin under his hands, hear the sounds she made as she came...

"Malax? Malax?"

Airen's sharp voice snapped him out of his daydream. He looked up to find her watching him with narrowed eyes.

"You're thinking of her, aren't you?"

"What?"

"The Terran, Wren." Airen's lips firmed. "She's clouding your head."

Malax stiffened. "No, I—"

"You've been obsessed with her ever since she came aboard."

He stood. "She hijacked my ship. Of course, I was focused on finding her."

"I know you, Malax. It's more than that."

Unease wound through him. "You think I'm neglecting my duties?"

"I think you're distracted."

He stared blindly at his desk. "I am dedicated to protecting everyone aboard this ship, including Wren." He met Airen's eyes, his gut churning. "If you're afraid of a repeat of Dalath Prime—"

His second-in-command hissed out a breath. "Of course not. But I'm your second, and it's my job to ensure your well-being. I'm also your friend, Malax." She leaned closer, voice lowering. "I know what haunts you, what drives you. You would never neglect your duty."

And yet Airen felt Wren was a distraction. *Cren.* He shoved a hand through his hair. She was right. Wren was all he could think about. He was so drawn to her.

But the faces of all his warriors on Dalath Prime moved through his head. The men and women who'd bled out on the planet's rocky surface, all because he hadn't seen the ambush coming. A young, cocky commander who'd been focused on too many things, except the ones that were most important.

He felt coolness wash over him. He needed to control this fascination with Wren and focus on his job.

There was a sharp rap at the door.

"War Commander? Second Commander?" A young

warrior stood in the doorway. "You're required on the bridge."

SLIDING OUT FROM UNDER A CONSOLE, Wren stood. She stretched her arms, nodding at the engineers who were just finishing up on the neighboring console.

Leaving her arms above her head, she bent her neck from side to side. She heard it crack and let out a sigh.

They'd done a lot of work. She looked down and saw she was grimy and dirty again. She was also tired.

But the thought of seeing Malax again was like a shot of adrenaline to the system.

The engineers had been great. It wasn't as great as being locked up alone in her computer lab back on Earth, but it had been interesting, complex work.

Calling out goodbyes to the engineers, she headed down the corridor.

Suddenly, she heard a distant boom. The *Rengard* shuddered violently and Wren was tossed into the wall.

Ouch. She straightened, spreading her feet as the ship jerked again.

"Sassy? What's happening?"

"It appears the *Rengard* is under attack."

Again? Wren started jogging toward the bridge. "By whom?"

"Long range weaponry belonging to the Kantos."

The fucking Kantos. They just never stopped attacking, swarming in like the bugs they were. She kept running, even when her lungs started burning. She finally made it to the bridge and stepped into controlled chaos.

Malax was the center of it. He stood, his hands clasped behind his back, directing his warriors to return fire. Airen stood beside him, her brow creased.

"What's happening?" Wren sucked in a deep breath.

They glanced her way.

"We finally got our longest-range scanners back on line," Airen said. "We discovered a huge swarm of Kantos ships not far from our location."

Wren gasped, looking at the viewscreen. *Shit.* This was her fault too. "They want the ship's helians."

Malax nodded.

"It is experimental technology that would enhance the Kantos' weaponry," Sassy added.

"We will not let that happen." Malax's tone held a hard edge.

As he barked out orders, Wren couldn't look away. He was so in control and commanding.

"The swarm is heading our way," Airen called out.

Wren studied the data on the screens. There were too many of them for the *Rengard* to fight off alone, and some of the Kantos ships were faster.

"We don't have many good options, Malax," Airen said. "We're caught between the Kantos and the Cra'nar Asteroid belt."

Frowning, Malax studied the screen. "We'll use the asteroid belt to lose them."

Gasps erupted around the bridge. Wren frowned, looking at all the impassive faces. Seriously, these warriors were good at hiding their emotions. "What's that?"

It was Airen who answered. "It's an asteroid belt."

Wren resisted rolling her eyes. "I got that much, but why the panic?"

Airen stiffened. "Eon warriors do not panic."

Wren pulled in a calming breath. "Fine. Why the concern?"

"The asteroids are metallic and volcanic," Sabin said.

Swiveling, Wren saw the images appearing on the viewscreen. She saw the dense asteroid belt ahead. "So they spew molten metal?"

"Correct," Malax said. "Molten iron to be precise. Over time, collisions with other asteroids has stripped away any rocky layers, leaving behind the dense metallic core."

"A molten core," Airen added. "They are covered with volcanoes that erupt with molten iron."

"That sounds...bad," Wren said.

"Molten metal landing on your ship is not a good thing," Sabin replied.

The man didn't even change facial expression. "You appear to be a master of understatement."

"We can get through," Malax said. "And it is unlikely the Kantos will follow us in there."

The atmosphere on the bridge turned tense. Wren clutched her hands together, watching and waiting.

"The Kantos are gaining," a warrior called out.

"And we are approaching the outer edge of the Cra'-nar," Airen murmured.

Wren wanted to grab Malax's hand, but right now, he was the cool, collected war commander.

"Sir, the lead Kantos ships will reach us before we're in the asteroid belt," another warrior called out.

Another image showed the incoming Kantos swarm. She saw the cluster of ugly, bug-like cruisers and smaller swarm ships.

Malax cursed under his breath. She saw the muscles straining in his neck.

Another volley of fire hit the *Rengard*.

"Brace," someone yelled.

Wren was rocked hard, almost falling. She staggered two steps and grabbed the light table. Next to her, Airen was swiping and tapping on the table.

No. She wasn't letting the Kantos destroy the *Rengard,* or get their dirty claws on any helians, or hurt anyone aboard. She whipped out her tablet and set it on the light table.

"Sassy?"

"Here."

"We need to get some more speed out of the *Rengard's* engines." She looked up and met Malax's gold-black eyes. He nodded.

"Assessing options now," Sassy said.

Wren touched the light table and the band on her wrist flared blue. She heard Airen make a choked noise, and then, Wren was connected to the *Rengard's* systems.

Holy cow.

As she thought of what she wanted, she saw data appear on the light table. And she no longer needed to tap or swipe. So. Cool. Excitement flooded her and she worked with Sassy, studying the *Rengard*'s systems.

"Sassy, funnel power from the environmental system to the star drives."

"That would put ventilation and heating at risk for the crew."

"I know, but it's feel dizzy and cold, or be dead."

Airen cleared her throat. "If you redirect the power from our storage areas, engine room, and docking bays, that would limit exposure for the crew."

Wren smiled. "Thanks. Do it, Sassy."

"Sir, power to the star drives has increased by thirty-three percent," a warrior at the helm cried out.

"Increase speed, Darnon," Malax ordered. "Get us into that asteroid belt."

The *Rengard* surged forward. Wren kept one eye on the star drives, monitoring the power situation, and her other eye on the giant asteroids looming ahead.

"Adjust course," Malax said. "Head for the center."

Wren studied the asteroids and bit her lip. *Oh, jeez.* They were huge and glowing. On several, she saw huge plumes of molten-red iron arching into space.

The molten metal would carve through the hull of the ship in seconds.

"Darnon, we need to avoid the plumes," Malax said.

The pilot was leaning forward in his seat, his gaze glued to his screen. "I'll do my best, sir."

"I believe I can help the pilot," Sassy said.

"Do what you can to enhance his systems, Sassy, but let him do his job," Wren murmured.

"Kantos are still coming," a warrior yelled.

The warship sailed between huge asteroids. The pilot turned them to the left, and ahead, Wren saw a large, irregular hunk of rock with an erupting volcano. The ship pulled up and she leaned into the light table. The *Rengard* was too big to be very nimble. Her mouth went dry. They might not make it.

"Rylan?" Malax called out.

"Kantos are still coming."

Malax cursed and Wren prayed the aliens would veer off.

Suddenly, the pilot cursed. "Plume!"

Alarms started blaring.

"We just caught the edge of it," Airen yelled. "We have a hull breach on deck delta-seven. Molten iron has torn into a cargo bay."

"Seal the breach," Malax ordered.

"Sealed."

"Sir," a warrior shouted. "The Kantos are retreating."

Cheers erupted. Wren released a shaky breath and when she looked up, Malax was watching her. She smiled, but he didn't return it. He nodded coolly before turning to his second.

"Airen, damage report."

"Just the one breach from the plume. It's sealed and I'll have repair crews down there shortly."

"Darnon?" Malax looked at the pilot.

"I've plotted the easiest course out of the asteroid belt. We should be clear in seven minutes and not encounter anymore eruptions."

"Good flying. Everyone, good work." Malax moved over to Wren. "Thank you."

She shrugged a shoulder. "I didn't do much."

"I'll be tied up here for some time." A rueful smile. "No time for dinner. I'll have Airen assign you a cabin so you can get some rest."

His face was cool and professional. There was no sign of the passionate man who'd given her the mother of all orgasms earlier. Her belly clenched. *Right.* Apparently, he'd had a change of heart since their moment in his cabin.

Or maybe he's just busy and has a job to do, Wren.

Either way, she wasn't going to make a fool of herself in front of all his warriors. She was done making a fool of herself over men.

"Okay, then. I need to retrieve my backpack anyway. Although, it's mostly just full of dirty clothes and empty wrappers."

He gave her a polite look.

She cleared her throat. "Right. Good luck." Her chest tight, she nodded and followed Airen out.

CHAPTER NINE

The next morning, Malax strode into the cargo bay. Repairs looked like they were going well.

The molten iron had burned a large tear in the side of the *Rengard's* hull, but as he watched, his repair crew climbed over the wall, welding and patching. A shower of sparks floated down to the floor. The ship's helians also helped enhance the repairs, growing new hull material to close the gap.

He swiped a hand over his face, feeling tiredness tug at him. He'd caught a few hours of sleep in his office off the bridge. With his ship in upheaval, there had been too much to monitor and check in on.

"They should have the bulk of the work finished over the next two shifts," Airen said from beside him.

He nodded. He'd been busy, but it hadn't stopped him thinking of Wren.

Or the flicker of hurt and confusion on her face when he'd all but ignored her on the bridge.

Malax rubbed his temple. He had a job to do. He had to keep reminding himself of that. Not this growing obsession with an Earth woman.

"You're thinking of her again," Airen said.

He speared his second with a look. "Don't start, Airen." He took a deep breath. "Do you know where she is?"

"With the engineers next door helping repair the cargo bay systems." Airen smoothed a hand down her braid. "There is no doubting that she's talented with a comp and equipment."

"Yes."

"We're a day away from reaching the *Desteron*."

And then she'd be gone. Malax stayed silent, his gut turning into a hard knot.

Airen paused. "Her helian, Sassy..."

"One problem at a time, Airen. We'll deal with Sassy later."

His second nodded. "I'll be on the bridge if you need me."

Malax walked along the line of repairs, then strode through a doorway to the neighboring cargo bay. A wall of sound hit him, music blaring through the bay.

It wasn't like any music he'd heard before. His gaze fell on Wren, who was swinging her hips to the music as she held her tablet. She looked at one of the engineers and raised a thumb at the man.

"You like it?" she called out to him.

"Earth music is...lively," the engineer said.

Then Wren turned and spotted Malax. A huge smile broke out on her face.

Malax felt it in his gut. He didn't smile back, just nodded. "Thank you for helping with the repairs."

Her smile slipped. "Sure. Did you get any sleep?"

"A little. It's been busy."

She tucked a curl back behind her ear. "Well, let me tell you, my first night in a real bed was *awesome*."

He wanted to smile, to touch her, to hold her. But instead, he forced himself to recite the names of his lost warriors on Dalath Prime.

"I'll leave you to your work. We have a day until you'll be back with your sisters."

He saw her face fall, the spark bleeding out of her eyes.

Gritting his teeth, Malax turned and headed for the doorway. Halfway there, he heard a strident beep.

"Malax, wait up."

Turning, he saw Wren rushing over to him. She was staring at her tablet and about to trip over a pile of tools. He caught her arm before she fell.

"Oops, thanks."

He felt the heat of her and instantly, his body responded. "What is it?"

Her brow was creased. "Sassy is picking up a heat signature in the conduits. It isn't any of your warriors and —" she sucked in a deep breath "—it looks like it's headed toward the helian core."

His pulse jumped and he looked at her tablet screen. He saw the glowing blotch of color on the map and touched his communicator.

"Airen? Wren is picking up a heat signature in the conduits. Run a scan."

"On it," Airen replied. "There is nothing showing on scans."

"No bio-signatures? No Kantos?"

"I'm running the scan again."

Wren bounced on her toes, her teeth biting into her bottom lip.

Stay focused, Dann-Jad.

"Nothing," Airen said again.

"Thanks." He met Wren's gaze. "It must be a false alarm."

"I do not do false alarms," Sassy snapped.

He kept his gaze on Wren's face. "Thank you for your help, but my team have confirmed the scans are clear. We know our ship better than anyone."

Wren pressed her tongue to her teeth. "Are you going to pat me on the head now and tell me to have a nice day?"

He stilled. "What?"

"I'm not really liking this cool, distant version of you."

"This *is* me."

She shoved a hand on her hip. "It isn't the man I've gotten to know the last few days."

"That man has been distracted by you, and he has a job to do."

Her head jerked. "So, I'm a distraction now. Right."

He curled his hands into fists. "Wren—"

She shook her head, her curls flying. "No, I get it. I'm a distraction, I've messed up your orderly ship, and I don't belong here."

Malax didn't respond.

Wren sucked in a breath and he saw the glimmer of wetness in her eyes. It was like a blow to his stomach. He lifted a hand to reach for her, but she quickly stepped back.

"God, why is my douche-radar so broken?" she muttered.

"I can't afford to lose focus, Wren. Lives depend on me doing my job."

Alarms started blaring and Airen's voice cut through their tense conversation.

"Malax, Wren was correct. I recalibrated the scanners to scan more than just bio-signatures or Kantos. There is *something* near the helian core, but it isn't biological."

Malax cursed, his gaze met Wren's again.

Then together, they sprinted out of the cargo bay.

WREN AND MALAX ran down a corridor. The thunder of boots came from a side corridor, and Sabin and his security team joined them.

Sabin held a small scanner. "We're close."

"Get us in there, Sabin," Malax said.

"Here." Sabin thumped a conduit cover in the wall.

Malax gripped it and ripped it off. Sabin and his warriors rushed in first. Malax went next, and Wren followed. As they hurried through the tight space, she managed to thump her elbow on the wall.

Ow. Malax turned and grabbed her arm.

She pulled away and brushed past him. He'd called her a distraction and given her the cold shoulder. She was equal parts pissed and hurt. Dammit, she barely knew the man. He shouldn't affect her like this.

Turning sideways, she squeezed through a narrow part of the maintenance conduit. At least she wasn't crawling.

Then Sabin and his team came to a halt. Curses filled the space. When the warriors shifted, she saw the conduit ended, and ahead was a small, horizontal tunnel. It was too small for Eon warriors, but not for a Terran woman.

Yay, more crawling.

Wren shoved forward.

"Wren, no." Malax gripped her shoulder.

"Whatever it is, we have to stop it before it reaches the helian core," she said.

Malax looked away and muttered something.

"We can circle around," Sabin said. "The tunnel opens up again not far from the core."

"I'll try to slow it down until you get there," Wren said.

Malax grabbed her arms again. "You stay safe. Don't take any risks."

His face was filled with emotion, the strands of gold in his eyes glowing, and she felt something in her chest crack. "See you soon."

Turning, Wren got crawling. Thankfully, the tunnel wasn't too long. Being cautious, she climbed out the other end into an octagonal-shaped room. Several conduits opened up onto the space.

"Weird alien signature, where are you hiding?" she whispered.

"Incoming from the left," Sassy said.

Wren swiveled, just as a...thing came out of the doorway of another tunnel.

She blinked. It didn't look like anything she'd ever seen before. It was about the size of a dog and made entirely of gray, shiny metal spikes. It looked like a bunch of metal shards had stuck to a magnet and started walking around. It turned in her direction and stopped.

"The creature is an iron-based lifeform," Sassy said.

"Seriously?" She'd heard that SpaceCorps had a record of some non-carbon-based lifeforms they'd encountered, but she'd never seen one before.

"Be careful, Wren, it is sentient, and its core temperature is extremely hot."

Okay. She held out a palm. "Nice alien."

The alien darted toward her and Wren backed up a step. It rushed her again, aiming for her legs. She squeaked and she kicked it.

It scuttled backward, its metal spikes quivering.

Uh oh.

Before it rushed at her again, there was a thumping sound and a wall panel nearby vibrated. Wren sucked in a breath and then the metal tore open and Malax's big body burst through. He was wearing his black armor.

His gaze fell on the metal creature and a sword formed on his arm. "Xukra."

"You know what it is?"

"An iron-based lifeform from the planet Xukrana.

They live in seas of molten iron. Highly aggressive and very dangerous."

Wonderful. The alien bristled and Malax attacked.

She watched them circle each other and Malax slashed at it with his sword. Then the Xukra leaped into the air, aiming for Malax's throat. The next swing of his sword cut the alien in two.

It fell to the floor and Wren saw the glowing, red-hot insides of the alien.

"They are an ally of the Kantos," Malax said.

Something clicked inside her head. "Oh, God, the Kantos *wanted* us to enter that asteroid belt."

Malax nodded, face grim. "They had Xukra in the molten iron on the asteroids, waiting to board the *Rengard.* This came aboard through the damage to the cargo bay."

"To try and get the helians," she finished.

"Yes, the Kantos are proving to be more cunning than the Eon High Command guessed. For years, they've just swarmed, with little strategy, but now..."

Suddenly, the sound of metal scraping on metal made them both turn. The Xukra's severed parts vibrated, then snapped back together.

What the hell? Wren backed up a step. She watched in horror as the alien started increasing in size, its spiky shards multiplying.

"Wren!" Malax dived at her, taking her to the ground.

She hit hard, with most of his weight on top of her. Her tablet went flying out of her hands and the air rushed out of her. Then she saw metal shards whizz over their heads. The deadly projectiles sliced into the wall behind them.

Shit. Her pulse jumped. If those hit their skin…

"Crawl." Malax urged her up on her hands and knees.

More shards shot from the Xukra. As Malax used his sword to deflect them, Wren crawled toward the closest conduit.

"Go." Malax was right behind her. "Move faster."

She scrambled into the conduit. Damn, they needed somewhere to hide. She spotted a panel down low and quickly yanked it open. Beyond it was a tiny space, only about a meter high.

"In here." She ducked inside and a second later, Malax moved in behind her.

Suddenly, the small space got very cramped. He rammed the panel closed, locking them in the darkness. She was plastered against his body and he was bent over to fit in the space. The sound of their breathing echoed in the tight confines.

Then she heard a metallic clanking outside.

The Xukra was *right* outside their hiding place.

Wren reached for Malax's hand. His fingers closed around hers and squeezed.

Then a glow flared in the darkness. She heard Malax curse.

"What?" she whispered, shifting to see past his broad back.

The panel was glowing red around the edges.

Her eyes widened. "What's it doing—?"

Malax kicked at the panel. It didn't budge. He kicked again and again.

"*By Ston's sword.*" With a final, frustrated slam of his boot, he slumped back. "The Xukra welded the panel shut."

Her heart lodged in her throat. "So, we're—"

"Trapped."

CHAPTER TEN

"Sabin? Airen?" Malax's communicator stayed stubbornly quiet.

"Sassy?" Wren tapped the blue band on her wrist. "God, I hope my tablet is okay."

"My warriors will find us." He shifted, feeling very cramped in the small space. "It might be more comfortable if we lie down."

They maneuvered around, and with each brush of her body against his, Malax felt desire ignite. She pressed her hand to the floor, right between his legs, brushing his thigh.

"Oh, damn, sorry." She pulled her hand away and finally managed to lie down on her side. Malax shifted as well, spreading out to face her.

Their gazes locked in the dim light from her wristband and his armor.

Then they heard running footsteps and shouting in the conduit outside. Malax heard the sounds of fighting.

He kicked the wall. "Sabin! In here."

"Malax?" Sabin's muffled voice.

"The Xukra trapped us in here."

There was the sound of banging, then it stopped. "The panel is welded shut, we'll need some tools." The sound of more shouting and fighting. "Malax, the Xukra is headed for the helian core—"

"Go!" Malax ordered. "Wren and I are fine. Stop the Xukra, then come back for us."

"I'll be back."

Soon the sounds of the fighting and footsteps faded.

"You think they'll catch it?" she asked.

"Yes. The Xukra can't survive in cooler temperatures for extended periods of time. They'll catch it or keep it from leaving." The Kantos were getting too bold and Malax didn't like it. Especially not on his ship. "The Kantos will *never* get my ship's helians."

Wren shifted and bumped her head on the top of their hiding place. "Ouch."

He reached out and helped her lower back down to the floor. He gently rubbed her head and watched as she went still and wary. Her pretty scent filled the space, seeping deep into his senses.

"I can't ignore you," he murmured.

Her chin lifted. "That's what you were trying to do? Because I'm a distraction?"

"I'm sorry."

"If you don't want to be around me, just say so, Malax, I—"

"I do want to be around you. That's the problem. That's all I want, all I think about."

Her chest hitched.

"I like touching you." He stroked the side of her face and heard her breath hitch again. "I like looking at you, hearing your voice, I want to see your smile."

Because he couldn't stop himself, Malax dropped a kiss to her lips. He kept it light, gentle, torturing himself with the taste of her. Her tongue darted out and licked his lips.

He groaned.

"No one's ever said anything like that to me before," she whispered.

He frowned. "Then the men of Earth must be stupid."

Her smile faded. "My parents mostly ignored me. I wasn't quick and athletic like my sisters." She moved a shoulder. "I was the geek among the badasses. And after my father died, I was invisible to my mother. Then there was this guy—"

Malax growled. "Who?" Did she love a man back on Earth?

Wren sighed. "My ex. He owned a gym, although his body was nothing like yours."

"Not a true warrior, then."

She giggled. "No. He liked to show off his physique, but I'm pretty sure Lance would run from a fight." Her face turned serious. "He cheated on me."

Malax grabbed her hand. How could any man not see what he had with a woman like Wren: beauty, strength, intelligence, love, and loyalty? "He was incredibly stupid."

"No, I was the stupid one. After I caught him, I realized how much he'd spoken down to me. He was always telling me not to eat that or to exercise more. *Dress more sexily, Wren. Don't talk about your work so much, Wren, it's boring.*"

"He was a jealous idiot. What did your sisters say about him?"

She nibbled on her bottom lip. "I never told them he cheated on me. They hated him from the beginning, and I didn't listen to them. I was embarrassed."

"Wren, we all make mistakes."

"You don't."

Every muscle in his body tensed. "I do. I have. Some that will haunt me forever."

Her gaze locked on his face. "Malax...?"

"On my first command mission, I lost warriors. I failed to listen to all the intelligence we had, I was arrogant, and my warriors died. I led them to their deaths."

Her small hand wrapped around his fist and she shifted closer. "It can't have—"

He shook his head. "I...can't talk about it." He couldn't tell her the bloody, gory details.

Suddenly, banging on the panel made them jerk apart.

"Malax," Sabin yelled.

"Sabin? Did you stop the Xukra?"

"We got it. Now, move back, we're going to cut you out."

WREN LET Malax help her out of the small crawl

space. Sabin and several warriors stood crowded in the conduit.

Malax cupped her cheeks. "Are you all right?"

She nodded. They all made their way back to the octagonal junction and when she saw the metallic shards embedded in the wall, she shivered. Then she spotted her tablet.

"Sassy!" She snatched the device up, checking it for damage. It looked intact.

"Are you okay, Wren Traynor?" Sassy asked.

"We're fine." She looked over and saw the warriors gathered around a frozen block of ice. Inside, she saw the remnants of the alien creature.

"We used coolant on the Xukra," Sabin said. "Once its body temperature goes too low, it ceases sentient functions."

"Excellent work, Sabin." Malax clapped the security commander on the shoulder.

"Sassy, any more of these Xukra aboard?" Wren asked.

"Negative. However, the *Rengard's* scanners appear to be malfunctioning periodically."

Malax shoved his hands on his hips. "I look forward to all my ship's systems being back to normal soon."

Sabin lifted his chin. "Airen suspects the Xukra did something to mess with the scanners. She has a team working on it."

"It was definitely after the helians," Malax said. "The Kantos are throwing everything they have at getting them." He eyed the frozen hunk of alien. "Record that and then get it off my ship."

The warriors circled the Xukra, readying to carry it off. Malax pressed a hand to Wren's back and led her out of the conduit.

As they stepped into the corridor, Wren pushed her hair back. "If I ever see any more maintenance conduits or vent tunnels, it'll be too soon."

"Wren." He tugged her to a stop. "Have dinner with me tonight. On the observation deck."

She bit her lip. "Are you sure that's a good idea?"

"Yes. It's my apology for trying to ignore you. I want to spend whatever time we have left together."

She dragged in a deep breath. "Okay."

His smile widened. "Good, that makes me very happy. I'll even have my chef prepare some Terran hot dogs."

She smiled at him. "I won't say no to a hot dog."

"Whatever is your pleasure, I'll do my best to give it to you."

Wren shivered. Those simple words said in that sexy voice reduced her to a pile of quivering desire. What she wanted most had nothing to do with food.

He tugged on one of her curls. "Now, I have to go."

Smiling, Wren watched him go. "Try not to fight any more aliens while I'm gone."

"Try not to hijack any other alien ships before I see you," he called back.

She was still grinning when she got back to her cabin. She tossed Sassy on the bed.

"Are you planning to have sexual intercourse with the war commander?" Sassy asked.

Wren choked. "What?"

"Are you planning—?"

"I heard you. It isn't polite to ask about someone's private life."

"Why?"

"Because it's private. And I have no idea what will happen with Malax." She dropped onto the edge of the bed. "I've never been so attracted to a man before...but he's an Eon warrior, I'm a Terran. And I'm leaving soon."

All that made her heart ache. She liked Malax, and for once in her life, he seemed to see her like no one else ever had.

"Sassy, synthesize me a fabulous dress while I have a shower." Another shower. *Yes*. She did a little booty shake on the way to the washroom.

Wren took her time bathing, drying her hair, then using some synthesized make up to enhance her eyes.

"Wren, the dress is in the synthesizer," Sassy said.

Wren pulled out a gorgeous length of purple fabric from the device. She stroked it, marveling at the silky feel. She tugged it on. It had a gold band at the collar that circled her neck, then the rich purple fabric cinched in at her waist and flared snugly over her hips. She ran her hands down it. She looked amazing, even if she did say so herself.

"I love it, Sassy."

"It accentuates your figure and the color suits your complexion."

And a certain warrior would love seeing her in it. Although, she was starting to think Malax didn't really care what she wore.

"One more thing before you leave," Sassy said.

"There is one more message for the war commander and I believe you should see it."

Wren huffed out a breath. "Sassy, you can't invade Malax's privacy like this."

The fancy Eon comp screen on the desk flickered to life and she groaned.

A woman's face appeared on the screen. A gorgeous Eon woman. Wren froze, her hands clenching on her purple dress. The woman was wearing some sort of twist of emerald silk that left one sleek shoulder bare. She had long, pale-brown hair. Miles of it. She was tall, toned, and beautiful, with lips painted a deep red.

Suddenly, Wren felt like she was wearing a sack.

"Hello, Malax." Her voice was a deep purr. "I hope you're well."

The woman stroked her neckline, down her collar-bone to her cleavage. What there was of it. Wren sniffed. At least Wren had the woman beaten in that department.

"I miss you so much," the woman continued.

Bile rose in Wren's throat. This sounded really personal. She opened her mouth to tell Sassy to stop the playback, but the woman continued to speak.

"I wanted to tell you that your mother is planning a commitment ceremony for us when you return to Jad." The woman smiled. Damn, she really was beautiful. "I know we're both terrible workaholics, and don't get to see each other much, but we enjoy each other's...company." The word was laced with innuendo. "When you're on Jad next, I'm hoping we can find the time to get married."

Married? Wren felt sick. "Turn it off, Sassy."

The screen froze on the woman's face.

"I thought you should see it." Sassy sounded subdued.

Wren let her mind go blank. The emotions churning inside her were rising up her throat. Was Malax a cheat? Had he made her a cheat too?

She sucked in a breath. No, this couldn't be right. Surely, she couldn't be so wrong about him?

She needed to talk to him. She glanced at the screen again and the woman's image.

Ugh. Yes, she needed to be an adult and communicate with him, but right now, she felt like vomiting. *God.* She felt like she had when she'd walked in on Lance with his pants around his ankles, humping Ms. Flexible and Bendy.

Wren's stomach did some horrible somersaults. She couldn't talk to Malax yet. She needed to regroup.

"It's okay, Wren." She took a few deep breaths and imagined punching the Eon woman in her perfect face. "I bet she can't create kickass computer programs and invent top-of-the-line computer components."

Wren methodically stripped off her dress, and in her head, she imagined sending a nasty computer virus all the way to the woman's computer on Jad.

Of course, Malax had a beautiful woman back on his home world. A tall, built Eon woman. Why wouldn't he? Maybe there was even more than one. The thought was depressing.

"Wren?" Sassy asked quietly.

Wren yanked on a clean set of black trousers and a shirt. "I'm not going to dinner."

"I shouldn't have shown you."

"It's fine, Sassy. I just need some time alone."

"Don't leave me here!"

Wren closed the door to her cabin and headed off down the corridor. She didn't really know where she was going. Pressing a palm to her forehead, she took another deep breath.

Eve and Lara would tell her to get all her facts first and confront the problem head on. But Wren wasn't like her sisters. She liked to think things through and sort out her emotions before she acted.

She turned a corner and heard a scraping sound.

Wren slowed, looking back over her shoulder. The corridor was empty.

Shaking her head, she kept moving.

She heard the sound again, and she spun. This time, she gasped.

A Kantos soldier stood in the center of the corridor. On its four powerful legs, it damn near blocked the entire space. Before she could react, it rushed forward, raising one of its sharp arms.

Fuck. She ran backward, tripped, and fell. The back of her head smacked against the metal grate floor. She saw stars.

She tried to push herself up, but she was dazed and dizzy.

A shadow blocked the light above her and she threw her arms up.

She saw the Kantos tilt its head, studying her. It held something clutched to its chest.

Wren saw what it was and gasped.

"No way!" The Kantos was holding a clear containment jar that was filled with blue fluid. Inside it was a glowing blue helian. The small creature looked like a slug and was pressed up against the glass.

Buzzing filled the corridor and she knew the alien was communicating with someone. Then the Kantos moved, scooping her up and tossing her over its bony shoulder.

"Let me go!"

The Kantos spun and moved fast down the corridor, its legs clunked on the metal as it ran. The up and down movement, combined with her fear, made her feel sick.

Think, Wren, think. "Sassy, if you are somehow monitoring me, I need help!"

There was no reply. She touched her wristband, hoping Sassy could hear her.

They moved through a dizzying array of corridors. Finally, the alien stopped and Wren knew they were near an external wall. A second later, she saw a shimmer and a hole was visible in the side of the hull. Beyond it, she saw a small, Kantos swarm ship. It was attached to the *Rengard's* hull.

Inside the ship was another Kantos soldier. A buzzing sound filled the air. They were communicating.

The soldier holding her stepped into the Kantos ship.

No.

Wren struggled against her captor. But then she received a sharp blow to her head, and everything went black.

CHAPTER ELEVEN

M alax fiddled with the plates on the table. He'd had the *Rengard's* chef put together food to suit a Terran palate, including the odd-looking hot dogs that Wren liked. The table was covered in plates and bowls of Eon delicacies, and he thought it looked rather...romantic.

He snorted. What did he know? He was an Eon war commander, and hadn't done anything romantic...well, ever. He turned to look out the large observation window. The view of the stars outside was the perfect backdrop. After spending most of the last week hidden in the bowels of his ship, he thought Wren would appreciate it.

The engineers had all the ship's systems operational, and they were back to moving at full speed. Airen had told him scanners were still not functioning at full capacity, but it shouldn't be long before that was fixed as well.

He tapped his fingers and wondered where Wren was. He frowned. She should have been here by now.

Malax kept staring out the window, and as more minutes ticked by, he realized he'd been stood up.

Had she not enjoyed the hot, sexy moments they'd shared? Was she still angry that he'd tried to avoid her? He'd thought of nothing but Wren and her soft curves all afternoon.

Annoyed with himself, he strode out of the observation deck and headed toward her cabin. Maybe she was still there? Maybe she'd fallen asleep?

He pressed the call button on her cabin door.

"Cabin is currently unoccupied," the computer intoned.

"Open the door." At his command, it whispered open and he stepped inside. It was empty.

Hands on his hips, he glanced around, sorting through the unfamiliar emotions inside him. The image frozen on the comp screen made him stiffen.

Jandala? He strode over and swiped the screen. His former lover's voice filled the room, along with her flood of *cren*-cursed lies. His gut hardened, anger filling him.

Wren had seen this.

After their kisses, after he'd pleasured her, she'd heard another woman talking about him and marriage. Gritting his teeth, he spun. He had to find her.

"Dann-Jad."

Sassy's distorted voice came from the bed. He turned and spotted Wren's tablet. *Cren*, from what he could tell, Wren didn't go anywhere without that tablet. "Sassy?"

"I'm giving you the benefit of the doubt—"

"You showed Wren the message from Jandala."

"She deserved to know."

He snatched up the tablet. "What you showed her *isn't* the truth of my life. Or how I feel."

The intelligence made a sound. "It isn't important right now. What is important is the fact that a Kantos soldier has snatched Wren."

"What?" Ice filled Malax's veins. "Where?"

"They have a small swarm ship attached to the hull on deck Delta-Seven. Hurry, warrior, they are preparing to leave."

Malax broke into a sprint, commanding his helian to form his armor. As the scales flowed over his body, he arrowed down a corridor, racing toward the deck Sassy had noted. He shoved Wren's tablet into his belt. He planned to give it back to her as soon as could. *Be okay, Wren.*

He tapped his communicator. "Sabin, we have Kantos aboard. They've taken Wren. Deck Delta-Seven."

Sabin's curses filled the line. "With the scanner compromised, they snuck aboard." More curses.

"What?" Malax barked, sprinting around a corner.

"They breached the helian core."

Dread rolled through Malax. "No."

"Malax," Airen said. "They have a helian. It looks like they managed to grab one before the other helians responded and used an electric shock to drive them out."

The Kantos had a helian and Wren.

Malax pushed himself for all the speed he had, running faster and harder than he ever had before.

Wren. He had to stop them from taking her.

It felt like an eternity before he broke out of a

doorway on deck Delta-Seven. Where was the Kantos ship? He searched the external wall.

His helian throbbed and he felt the increase in energy from one spot. He couldn't see the hole, as they'd clearly camouflaged it, but he could sense it.

"Malax, I'm one minute out with my security team," Sabin said.

"Wren doesn't have that long."

"Wait for backup!"

Malax ignored his security commander, sucked in a breath, and dived.

As he flew through the hull breach the Kantos had cut, he felt the prickle of energy over his body. His helian formed a helmet for him and then he was outside the *Rengard*. He landed on top of the Kantos ship and clung to it.

Now, he just had to get inside.

Then he felt the rumble of engines beneath him.

WREN WOKE, her head throbbing. *Where was she?*

Something smelled bad and she breathed through her mouth. A buzzing sound filled the air and she froze. *Kantos.*

She opened her eyes.

She was sprawled on the floor of a Kantos swarm ship. In front of her, two big Kantos soldiers were sitting in huge seats, in front of some sort of console.

Shit. What should she do? At least they hadn't left

yet. She could see the hull of the *Rengard* out the forward viewscreen, and they weren't moving.

Think, Wren. You need some sort of sensible plan, or your ass is getting kidnapped.

She must have made a sound, because both soldiers whipped their heads around. They pinned her with soulless stares, their four beady, yellow eyes like pinpoints of light.

Her mouth went dry.

We detect a helian signature on you.

The voice echoed in her head. *Crapola.* That had to be Sassy's wristband. Wren barely resisted the urge to slap her hand over the blue band. Fingers crossed they thought it was jewelry.

"I don't know what you're talking about."

Your heart rate has increased. That indicates you are lying.

"I'm clearly not Eon. I don't have a helian." She looked over and saw the containment jar locked into place on a built-in shelf. Thank God they'd only managed to nab one.

Suddenly, an ugly, screeching sound ripped through the cockpit. Wren blinked, watching as the soldiers frantically turned back to the console. She realized it was an alarm.

The buzzing sounds increased.

"What's happening?" Wren yelled.

They didn't respond, but she guessed that the Eon had detected the swarm ship. She smiled. *Take that, bug boys.*

There was a vibration beneath her, and she felt like a

hand reached into her chest and squeezed. They'd started the swarm ship's engines.

Uh-oh. She scrambled to her feet. A second later, the Kantos ship took off, speeding into space.

Wren was knocked off her feet. She hit the floor and rolled across the back of the Kantos ship. She pulled herself up, looking out a small side window.

She watched the *Rengard* getting smaller and smaller.

No, no, no. She'd just been abducted by the Kantos, and no one knew.

MALAX CLUNG to the outside of the Kantos swarm ship as it raced away from the *Rengard*.

He pressed himself hard against the hull, his armor helping him cling to the side.

He scowled. The Kantos had better not have hurt Wren. Crawling toward the back of the small ship, he lifted his arm and slammed his fist against the metal. It dented. He kept hammering, his helian increasing the strength in his fist.

After a few more concentrated blows, he tore a hole in the ship, then dropped through, feet first.

He heard an alarm screeching, and a second later, the hull breach system sealed the hole behind him. Once he was steady, he stormed through the small ship. There was a door between him and the cockpit. He gripped it, and tore the door off with a screech of metal. He tossed it behind him.

He saw Wren swinging a box at a Kantos soldier's head. The alien leaped from his seat, spinning to attack her.

Anger stormed through Malax.

They'd stolen her. They'd tried to snatch his woman away. If Sassy hadn't warned him....

With a growl, Malax strode forward, his sword forming on his arm. The second Kantos soldier rose, and leaped at him. Malax gripped the Kantos, slashed down with his sword, and sliced through one of its arms. He threw the soldier into the wall.

He followed through, skewering the alien and ensuring he was dead.

Malax swung around and saw Wren stagger back, clutching her arm. The other soldier had hit her.

"They've got a helian," she warned.

She pointed behind him and Malax saw the shatter-proof container filled with blue fluid. He saw the helian floating inside.

You cannot stop us.

Malax's gaze moved to the final Kantos. An elite—one of the leaders of the soldiers. "Yes, I can. Down, Wren."

Instantly, Wren dived to the side, rolling out of his way.

Malax charged the elite and the Kantos rushed to meet him. They collided, hard. Wrestling, Malax fought to avoid the Kantos' flailing arms and legs. They were too close for him to get his sword in the right position.

With a grunt, he strained against the alien. They bounced off the pilot's chair and slammed into the command console. They wrestled some more, shoving and grunting. Part of the console crumpled under their weight, discordant alarms filling the cockpit.

The Kantos shoved Malax back. He used the momentum, raised his sword and threw himself forward.

His blade rammed through the Kantos' hard gut.

The elite's eyes flared brightly, then faded. He slumped, and Malax wrenched back his sword.

Then the ship lurched to one side and he staggered. Behind him, he heard Wren curse. He commanded his sword to dissolve.

Alarms were screaming, and he saw that the ship was out of control. And part of the console was destroyed.

Wren appeared, clutching his arm. "Can you fly this?"

"Yes."

She blew out a breath. "Thank God."

He yanked her close, pulling her up on her toes. *By Eschar's bow*, he was glad she was alive. He gave her a fast kiss.

When he released her, she looked dazed. *Good.* He sank into the pilot's chair and started touching the controls on the non-ruined side of the console.

First, he tried to contact the *Rengard*. Nothing. *Cren*, the comms system was completely inoperable. He couldn't get any comm lines.

Wren sat in the seat beside him. "You can just turn us around and get us back to the *Rengard*, right?"

He touched the controls again. All Eon warriors were trained to fly various enemy craft. "No. The ship's controls are damaged. I don't have full flight control, and I can't communicate with the *Rengard*."

"Oh, God... And that's not good, is it?" She pointed at the viewscreen.

Malax leaned forward. Fluid was spewing out of the ship and into space.

Cren. He tapped the controls. "No, that's not good. That's fuel venting."

"Shittity, shit."

And it got worse. "And it appears we're also losing oxygen."

Wren's mouth dropped open. "You have any good news, warrior?"

He touched the screen, running some scans. "I just scanned for habitable planets. There's one not too far away."

Malax coaxed the controls, finally aiming the ship toward the orb that appeared on the screen. He pushed their beleaguered ship for everything it had.

If they took too long, they'd run out of fuel, or oxygen, or both.

"They snatched me," Wren said. "They'd clearly snuck aboard and got to your helian core."

"You're safe now."

She nodded. "You get us on the ground, and the *Rengard* will eventually find us."

"Yes. The ship's systems are damaged, so our landing won't be gentle."

Her face turned white. "Oh, God, we're going to crash!"

"Crash is a strong word. A rough landing."

She pulled the straps over her shoulders. "You say tomato, I say tah-mah-to."

He frowned at her. "What?"

She waved a hand. "Earth saying. Please, carry on ensuring we don't smash into a fiery ball of death and destruction."

Malax concentrated on piloting the swarm ship. The green planet rose up ahead of them, filling the viewscreen.

"What planet is this?" she asked.

"An old abandoned planet. It's too far from any occupied sectors to be of interest." He tapped the Kantos screen, attempting to translate the scrawl of their language.

They hit the atmosphere, and things got rough. He heard Wren moan.

With the ship rattling and shaking, both of them pressed back into their seats and he flew them lower. They broke out of the clouds, and he saw trees spread out beneath them. The screen flashed information: temperate climate, with forests, lakes, and inland sea.

He saw a crescent of yellow sand, with waves crashing up against a wall of dark cliffs nearby.

And on top of the cliff, he saw ruins.

"Oh, wow," Wren murmured.

The ancient ruins spread in a vast ruined city.

Another alarm screeched, hurting his ears. "We're coming in fast. Are you strapped in?"

"Yes. Please get us down safely. I'll give up chocolate, sex, anything."

He glanced her way. "I'll make sure you don't have to

give up any of that." Then he studied their landing options. Water would be best. He aimed the ship, and they raced toward the sea.

Wren whimpered. She gripped her armrest, staring out the viewscreen.

"Close your eyes," he said.

"I can't." She dragged in a breath. "Let's do this."

They hit the water with a giant splash. Wren screamed, and they were both tossed violently against their harnesses.

They skidded across the water. Gritting his teeth, Malax kept his hands on the controls, trying to retain some control of the ship.

Racing toward the land, he tried to keep them aimed for the sand, and not the vicious, sharp rocks at the base of the cliffs. Suddenly, they hit the beach, sand spraying up in front of them. They jerked to a hard stop, their bodies flung forward in their harnesses one last time.

Malax dropped back against his seat and released a harsh breath.

They were down.

CHAPTER TWELVE

W ren felt sick. She was pretty sure her stomach was tied up like a pretzel.

She also felt dizzy. She pushed her hair out of her face and looked up at the viewscreen.

Sand and trees filled her vision. They'd crash-landed, but they were alive.

Malax looked at her and smiled. "Not bad." He tore his belt off, then reached over and helped her with hers.

Suddenly, the pretzel in her belly unraveled. She wrenched away from him and raced for the door. "Open it!"

The door slid open and she raced outside. She took two steps, dropped to her knees on the sand, and started retching.

A strong hand slid into her hair, holding it back from her face.

Great. Wren vomited again. Mid-heave, she had the crazy thought that she bet Malax's gorgeous fiancée had never vomited her guts up in front of him. If she had, she'd probably looked beautiful while she'd done it.

Wren, on the other hand, felt like she'd been inside a clothes cleaner and then spat out, still wet and tangled.

Once her stomach was empty, Malax pulled her back against his big body. She was too exhausted to move away.

"The water is safe to drink," he said.

Thankful, she leaned over to where the gentle waves were lapping up onto the sand. She scooped up some water to her lips. Unlike on Earth, this ocean wasn't salty. She rinsed out her mouth, then took a long drink of water.

Finally, she sagged back against Malax and leaned into his strength. She took a moment to look around. It was a beautiful planet. The temperature wasn't hot or cold, the beach looked pristine, and the nearby trees were a mix of green, red, and purple.

And looming above them, at the top of the cliff, were those fascinating ruins.

"Now what?" she asked.

"We wait for the *Rengard* to find us."

"They *will* find us, right?"

"Yes. I alerted Sabin when I went after you. They'll run searches and find the trail of the Kantos ship. It might take some time, but neither Airen nor Sabin are known for giving up."

Suddenly, Wren's stomach grumbled.

"I owe you dinner," Malax said.

Dinner. Right. She shot him a faint, forced smile.

He tipped her chin up. "I know you saw the message from Jandala."

Wren winced. God, she didn't want to know the woman's name. "Sorry. Sassy showed it to me." God, she hated this. Her stomach felt sick again. "Your fiancée seems...nice."

"She's not my fiancée." He scowled. "She has expressed the wish to marry me numerous times, and numerous times, I stated my lack of interest in making that happen."

"Mmm."

"Wren." He cupped her cheek. "I'm not engaged to her. I haven't made a commitment to another woman, and I haven't seen Jandala in months." His fingers stroked her cheek. "I assure you that I've been blindsided by a clumsy, smart, beautiful Terran who hijacked my warship."

Everything inside her went still, then heat flashed through her. "Really?"

"Really."

They stared at each other, locked in the moment.

"I have something for you." Malax rubbed his thumb down her cheek.

"Oh?"

He pulled something off his belt and held it up.

"Sassy!" Wren grabbed it, holding it tightly to her chest. "Thank you."

Another soft stroke of his thumb. "Time for dinner."

All she could do was nod.

He helped her to her feet and they went back inside the Kantos ship. The smell hit her again and she breathed through her mouth. She watched as he stacked the bodies of the Kantos soldiers in a storage compartment at the back of the ship, dragging them by one leg. *Ugh.* She looked away, not wanting to see them, or the green blood pooling on the floor beneath them. She heard him slam the door closed.

"Don't want any wildlife sniffing around in here," he said.

Double ugh. "Um, is there any wildlife that's going to try and eat us?"

A smile tilted his lips. "Scans didn't show anything dangerous on land, and my helian will warn us if anything gets too close."

Malax checked on the helian in the containment jar. It appeared to be safe inside its container, happily unaware of all the chaos around it. Next, he grabbed some gear and they headed back outside.

Even though it was dinnertime for them, it appeared to be the middle of the day on the planet. She watched him head closer to the trees and break some branches off a tree. He snapped them into smaller pieces and expertly began making a small fire.

Thank God he had skills, because if Wren had been the one who needed to make a fire, they would have been out of luck.

Next, he laid out the blanket he'd taken from the Kantos ship. It was mud-brown and looked like it was made from some sort of hide. At least it looked clean. He pulled over a fallen log to act as a seat.

"Is it safe to pick some fruit?" she asked.

He nodded. "And there appear to be some crustaceans in the water. I'll see what I can catch."

Wren wandered to the trees where she'd spotted some round, fat fruits. She thumbed her tablet screen. "Sassy?"

"Wren! You and the war commander are okay? I detect that you're on an alien planet."

"We're fine."

"I am very pleased to hear that." A pause. "I feel that showing you that message set all this in motion—"

"It's fine," Wren said. "We sorted things out. We're going to wait for the *Rengard* to find us." Spotting some fruit, Wren plucked what she could reach from the lowest branches. "Can you run some scans, Sassy? Check out the wildlife and those ruins on the cliffs."

"Certainly."

"Other than that, do *not* scan my vitals." Wren swiveled, her gaze falling on Malax. He splashed in the water, catching some crab-like animals with an ease she admired.

"Very well, Wren. I'll lay low."

Wren rolled her eyes. She was pretty sure Sassy had no idea how to lay low.

Tucking her tablet away, Wren collected some more fruit. The bit of exertion made Wren feel warm, and she unzipped her shirt a bit. Soon, they were sitting around the fire, the crabs roasting, and both of them munching on the strange, round, green fruit she'd collected. They tasted weird, but sweet.

"So, the Kantos really wanted a helian from the *Rengard*," she said.

Malax nodded. "They've been attempting to experiment with helians." His brows were drawn together. "They want to replicate Eon technology." Deep anger vibrated in his voice. "They don't understand the symbiotic relationship we have with the helians. We offer the helians the chance to live, to challenge themselves and their abilities, and in return, we protect them and never force them to do what they do not want to do. The Kantos give no thought to the wellbeing of the helians as they try to make their weapons. If the Kantos succeed in getting their hands on our tech, they'd be unstoppable."

They were pretty darn unstoppable as it was. Wren wiped her sticky hands on her trousers. "We have to stop them getting any more helians. If they get Eon tech, they wouldn't just destroy Earth, they'd come after the Eon planets next." They'd try to decimate the galaxy. "Bloody Kantos."

"Agreed." Malax held a succulent bit of crab out for her.

She nibbled on it and the smoky flavor burst in her mouth. *Yum.* She took her time, enjoying the flavors. He kept passing her other little tidbits of fruit and crab.

Desire was a low burn in her belly. He was sitting right beside her, so big, strong, and handsome. His leg kept brushing hers. He'd leaped onto the outside of a Kantos ship for her. He'd come for her and rescued her.

Wren shifted on the log, rubbing her thighs together. When she glanced up, she froze. His hungry gaze was on her. The gold filaments in his eyes were glowing.

The next time he held some fruit out for her, she leaned forward and took it from him with her teeth. She licked his finger and heard him make a small sound. She sucked his finger into her mouth.

Malax groaned. "Wren."

"Malax."

He yanked her forward into his arms and his mouth crashed down on hers.

Oh. God.

She wrapped her arms around him, kissing him back. Their previous kisses had been amazing, but this one... *Hot. Rough. Intense. Pulse-pounding. Soul-shattering.*

Stop thinking, Wren. She opened her mouth and pulled him closer.

MALAX'S BLOOD HEATED.

He sat back on the log and lifted his head. Wren was panting, her eyes clouded with desire. So pretty and cute.

"Come here, *shara*," he murmured, pulling her up to stand in front of him.

"What's *shara* mean?" she asked.

"It's what one of the first Eon warriors, Alqin, called his mate Eschar."

He pulled her between his spread legs, his hands on her hips. He let his hands drift over her, exploring. He pushed the hem of her shirt up and ran his hands over the smooth skin of her belly.

She rested her hands on his shoulders, her fingers kneading. He reached behind his neck and yanked his own shirt off.

Her eyes fell to his chest, going wide. She let out a

small moan. "You're perfect. Big. Ripped."

He met her gaze. "Ripped?"

"Muscular and in great shape. I'm *not* ripped."

"I know. I like it."

He lifted her hands and pressed them to his chest. Her fingers flexed on his skin, and she started to explore.

"Your skin is so hot." She took her time, molding his muscles, skimming her fingers over his shoulders. Each small move set fires off along his nerve endings. Then her hands moved downward, her nails scraping over his nipples.

He felt each touch in his cock and he groaned.

Then he reached up, tugging her shirt off. She went still and her breasts bobbed free.

"*Cren*, you're gorgeous." He cupped her breasts and took his time, watching the nipples turn into hard, little pebbles. He leaned forward and pressed his mouth to one.

"Oh, yes," she moaned.

Malax laved it with his tongue, then sucked it into his mouth. She let out a husky cry, her hands sliding into his hair. He wrapped an arm around her to keep her upright. He sucked deeply, enjoying the taste and feel of her.

Taking the time to enjoy her responses, he kept on pleasuring her. She whimpered, squirming against him.

"Malax, that feels so good."

He lifted his mouth, blowing on her damp skin. Then he let his hands drop down to her trousers, quickly unfastening them. He pushed them down, watching as he uncovered the pale skin of her legs. His gut clenched tight with desire. He couldn't get enough of her.

Need was pounding inside him. He let his hands drift up her legs, stroking the inside of her thighs. She trembled.

"Pretty." He let one hand delve between her legs and stroked her.

He'd touched her like this before, but he hadn't been able to look at her, or fully taste her.

Malax slid a finger inside her, and she made a choked, husky sound. He looked up her sweet body, his gaze locking on her face. He could read everything she was feeling on her features. Wren never hid what she was feeling. Her cries echoed around the beach.

"I want my mouth on you, Wren."

"Oh...well, don't let me stop you."

He surged upward, taking her with him. He lifted her, then set her down on the blanket he'd laid out for them. He dropped down and rolled onto his back. He pulled her on top of him so that she was straddling his chest.

She looked startled. "What are you—?"

"I want you straddling my face."

Her eyes went huge. "Oh. *Oh*."

He gripped her hips and lifted her. She barely weighed anything. He pulled her until her thighs covered his ears, and those pretty pink folds were right in front of his eyes.

Malax breathed her in. His senses filled with Wren, with her sweet arousal. He wanted to pleasure her, wanted to hear her call out his name. His cock throbbed painfully.

He gripped her hips.

"Malax, maybe—"

He licked her.

She cried out, body jerking. He held her in place, using his tongue, lips, and teeth to pleasure her. She tasted like honey, and soon, she was moving, riding his mouth.

"Don't stop," she begged.

Cren, the sounds she was making were driving him crazy. Blood pounded through his body, and his stiff cock was pressed hard against the front of his trousers.

But this was about Wren's pleasure.

He sank his hands into the curves of her ass, urging her on. He'd never get enough of her taste. He was starving for her.

"Malax...oh God, I'm—"

She ground down on him and screamed, coming hard.

As she shuddered, he clamped his hands on her. He felt every shimmer of pleasure running through her. When she collapsed, still shuddering, he reared up and caught her.

Spinning, Malax laid her down, and then yanked his trousers open. He stood, shoving them down. His swollen cock sprung free.

Her eyes went straight to his cock. "Oh, wow. You're big."

"Yes, *shara*. But you can take me."

He was desperate now, and he quickly spread her legs, covering her body with his. She wrapped her arms around his shoulders, her nails digging into his skin. She urged him closer. Of course, his Wren wouldn't be nervous or afraid.

"Yes," she murmured. "Come inside me."

He rubbed his cock against her folds. "Are you sure you're ready?"

"Malax, we've been engaged in foreplay ever since I hijacked your ship." She rubbed against him. "If I got anymore ready, I'd combust."

He pushed inside her.

Wren let out a long breath and writhed beneath him. "Oh man." Her voice was breathy. "Really big."

"Relax, you can take all of me."

"Hell yes, I can." She gripped his back, urging him on. "I'm good at everything I do."

Smiling, he pulled away, then thrust back in. A groan ripped out of him. She was so tight and wet. He pulled back, and thrust in again, going a little deeper. On his next thrust, he was in, all of his cock lodged inside Wren's warmth.

Malax sank back on his knees, sliding his hands beneath her ass and lifting her. Seeing her beneath him, her body stretched around his cock, was the prettiest sight he'd ever seen.

"Malax, *move.*"

He started thrusting. "Hold on."

Her hips bucked up against him, and he gripped her harder. The last thread of his control snapped.

He started moving inside her with heavy, pounding thrusts.

"Yes. God." She threw her head back, her cries echoing down the beach.

CHAPTER THIRTEEN

W ren gripped onto Malax as he moved inside her.
He filled her—completely, thoroughly—
with each thrust. He was deep inside her, and she loved
his big body covering hers, owning hers.

Their gazes met. The heat in his eyes left her feeling
scorched. With each thrust, her breasts rocked, and hard
pleasure careened through her.

She'd never had sex like this before. She *loved* it.

He dropped his head and kissed her. His hips started
moving faster, and his big cock was stretching her, hitting
spots that made every nerve ending come to life.

Her next orgasm hit her suddenly, like an explosion.
"Malax!"

As pleasure swamped her, he kept pounding into her,
his grunts echoing in her ears.

"Feel it, Wren. Take it all."

She held onto him, feeling like a boat caught in a
wild storm.

There was a heavy groan, and Malax came. His big body shook, his cock pulsing inside her.

Finally, he rolled to the side, pulling her closer.

God, she was wrecked. In the best way ever. She looked up at the blue sky and decided she had to just stay like this forever, because she'd never be able to move again.

"You okay?" he rumbled.

"No," she said. "I'll never walk again. And I want you to stay naked for the rest of your life. And I love your big cock."

He stared at her for a beat, then laughter burst out of him.

She licked her lips. "Clearly, two stellar orgasms have broken my filter... And I have no filter on a good day."

Malax kissed her nose. "With me, you can say whatever you want. And you can always tell me what you're feeling."

"I need food." Wren reached for her shirt.

"You do," he agreed. "So I can fuck you again."

She glanced his way as he rose, her gaze drifting to his muscular ass. He was completely comfortable with his nakedness. He shifted and she saw that his cock was still hard.

She licked her lips, her belly fluttering. "Okay."

Malax gathered the rest of the food they'd collected earlier. It would be night aboard the *Rengard*, and she was fatigued. They lounged on the blanket, eating. Malax kept her pulled tight against his body, stroking her skin—on her hip, her belly, the underside of her breast.

He was so big and handsome. Like a lion lounging around in the shade. The king of the jungle.

"How much longer until your warriors arrive?"

He looked into the sky. "I'd guess a few hours."

Wren nodded, licking the tangy juice of a red fruit off her fingers. She rose, attempting to be nonchalant about her own nakedness. She moved to the water's edge and washed her hands.

This place was paradise. She hoped none of the local wildlife was staring at her bare butt. She turned her head, looking up at the ruins on the cliff above.

From here, she saw a few structures clinging to the cliffside—tumbled ruins tangled with vines and covered with moss.

She wished she could explore them. She wondered what long-ago species had built it, and what had happened to them.

When she moved her head, her gaze fell on Malax. Her pulse jumped. He was sitting on the log again. Still gloriously naked.

"Come here," he growled.

That voice, and the hot look in his eyes, had desire licking at her insides.

She walked toward him, loving the way his gaze moved over her, leaving no doubt that what he saw turned him on.

"Stop there," he ordered.

Standing right in front of him, she obeyed. She shivered. Subconsciously, she arched her back, and watched his gaze go straight to her breasts.

Feeling bold, she lifted her hands and cupped them.

"You know how much I like your pretty breasts, don't you?" His voice was deep, edging on guttural.

She loved knowing she could turn this big, sexy man on so much.

"Now turn around," he ordered. "And show me that sweet ass."

Oh God. Her knees felt weak, but again, she obeyed. She felt him behind her, and he pressed a gentle kiss to the small of her back.

Wren sucked in a breath.

"Lean forward."

She quivered. If she did that, he'd have a clear view of everything.

"Wren."

Pulling in a breath, she obliged, tilting forward, knowing he was looking at her. She heard him groan, his hands sliding to her hips.

"Going to fuck you again now."

"Fine by me," she breathed.

"Sit down on me," he murmured. "Slow. I'll hold you."

She shifted back, and he helped lower her down to his lap. She gripped his thighs for balance.

"That's it," he said. "Lower yourself onto my cock."

God. She felt the thick head of his cock nudge her and she moaned.

He rubbed against her.

"Good, Wren. Now, sit down and take my cock deep inside your tight, little body."

She slowly sank down, her body stretching around his cock. Then she was balanced in his lap, her back pressed against his firm chest. She dropped her head back against his hard shoulder.

"So sexy and sweet." He murmured in her ear. His hand slid down her belly, then in between her legs. She raised her head to watch as he rubbed her clit.

Her body spasmed on his cock, and they both groaned.

"I need to move, Malax."

"Not yet." His voice was strained, his finger strumming her clit.

Even though he wasn't moving, Wren felt the pleasure growing. Her climax was building. She rocked on him, needing to move.

He growled. His hands gripped her hips, yanking her up. Then he pulled her down hard on his cock and she cried out.

"You want my cock? Show me how much."

Her hands digging into his thighs, Wren moved up and down. He helped, his hands gripped hard on her hips as he helped her gyrate.

It didn't take long, and soon she was crying out. Her release rushed through her like a giant wave that pulled her under.

Suddenly, Malax nudged her forward. She landed on her hands and knees on the blanket, and then his big body was covering hers. He thrust inside her again, and she screamed.

"Wren." He cursed, his fingers biting hard into her hips as his cock plunged inside her.

A second later, he lodged deep, and came with a roar.

Wren was panting, trying to come back down from

the stratosphere. She felt him press a kiss to the back of her neck. His arm was the only thing holding her up.

"I can't move," she said. "Even if your warriors arrived right now, I couldn't move to get dressed."

Malax growled. "My men will *never* see you naked."

He shifted and picked her up. She clung to him as he strode into the water. "Malax—"

He walked straight into the waves and, as the cool water hit her skin, she squealed. He smiled down at her, and she loved the possessive look in his eyes.

She liked the feeling of belonging to this hard, sexy warrior.

She liked it...way too much.

MALAX WOKE from a nap and smiled. The sun was still high in the sky, the light warm on his skin.

His smile widened. Wren was sprawled on top of him, fast asleep.

"Wren." He slid a hand up her naked back and into her hair.

She made a mumbling sound.

He watched her lift her head, and warmth hit his gut. He could wake up to that pretty, grumpy face every day of his life.

Shock reverberated through him at the thought. He'd never felt that way about a woman before. He'd never felt like this ever.

And now he was feeling it for the Terran woman who'd turned his world upside down.

He slid his hand onto her hip and squeezed. "We should get dressed. I suspect a shuttle from the *Rengard* will be here shortly."

She nuzzled into him. "Not my first choice of things to do, but I really don't want a scowling Airen or Sabin to catch me naked."

Malax stroked her back. "They aren't so bad, and they're excellent warriors."

"They're understandably pissed that I hijacked your ship and set all this in motion." She lifted her head. "Why aren't you?"

He rubbed a thumb over her lips. "I'm starting to think that you hijacking my ship is the best thing that's ever happened to me."

She pulled in a breath. "Malax."

He had to kiss her again. He dragged her up, taking his time with that mouth of hers. Then he gently slapped her ass. "Now, let's not get caught putting on a show for my warriors."

Nodding she rose, pulling her clothes on, still sleepy. They'd only had a few hours of sleep.

Malax made short work of pulling his own gear on, not taking his eyes off her. He watched those delicious curves disappear under her clothes, and vowed to spend some time worshipping them again soon. He glanced at the gentle ocean waves. He'd remember their time on this little paradise fondly, but he really wanted to see Wren in his bed.

Suddenly, he heard a noise behind them.

Tensing, he spun. It had come from the Kantos ship. He felt a warning throb from his helian.

"Malax?" Wren whispered, voice tense.

Without thinking, he commanded his symbiont and black scales formed over his skin. His short sword formed on his arm.

It could just be a curious animal, but he wasn't taking any chances. "Stay back."

He strode towards the ship, and heard the clattering sound of something being knocked over or dropped.

He also sensed a presence behind him and glanced back. Wren was right behind him, clutching a long stick in her hands.

Blowing out a breath, he shook his head. He didn't have time to argue with her. He turned back to the Kantos ship and had taken a few steps when a Kantos elite burst out of the door.

Cren. It had streaks of green blood all over it and a damaged arm. It was one of the pair he was sure he'd killed earlier. Clearly, over the last few hours, it had managed to regenerate and get out of the storage compartment.

Malax lunged, swinging his sword. The Kantos ducked, skittering back on its legs.

"He's got the helian!" Wren yelled.

Malax spotted the helian container clutched against the alien's hard chest.

Anger roared through him and Malax charged.

The Kantos dodged, swiping out with a sharp arm. As Malax blocked the blow, the soldier spun and darted past Malax. It raced toward Wren.

No. He watched helplessly as the alien aimed for her.

She swung her stick like a bat, and the Kantos snapped it with one hard hit.

With a roar, Malax leaped through the air. He landed right behind the Kantos, swinging his sword upward.

The Kantos moved fast. It spun and lifted its free arm. Something shot at Malax.

A sticky, web-like substance wrapped around Malax's leg. He tripped.

Cursing, he cut at the sticky, black substance.

He heard Wren cry out, and lifted his head. He watched the Kantos grab her and lift her off the ground. Despite her struggles, the alien pinned her to its side.

Then the Kantos elite turned and raced off, into the trees.

"No!" Malax finally cut himself free of the sticky web and leaped to his feet. He ran into the trees, crashing through the vegetation.

He had to get to Wren and the helian.

He followed the trail, pulling everything from his helian to follow the sound of the Kantos. He cursed himself. He should have ensured the cren-cursed elite was dead earlier. Sometimes, a heavily wounded Kantos elite appeared dead, their vitals slowed to nothing, and yet they could regenerate enough to survive.

Pausing, Malax listened. *There.* He turned and kept running. The Kantos soldier was running up the hill toward the ruins.

Malax lost the trail and paused. He could only hear the sound of birds, the wind, and the distant waves. Where the *cren* were they?

"Fuck you, you creepy asshole. You are ugly as hell!"

Adjusting course, Malax followed the sound of Wren's angry voice.

When he surged out of the trees, he saw that they were right at the edge of the cliff. To one side, the ruins rose up above them. An intact archway of stone was a gateway into the ruined city.

But right in front of him, the Kantos soldier was standing on the edge of the cliff. Down below, waves crashed against the sharp rocks at the base of the cliff.

The Kantos had the sharp edge of his arm held against Wren's throat. She was glaring at the alien.

In the Kantos' other claw, he held the helian container. The sunlight glinted off the glass.

"Let her go," Malax demanded.

Four burning yellow eyes glared at him. *Make your choice, Eon.*

Without warning, the Kantos shoved Wren off the cliff.

Her screams pierced the air, her arms and legs thrashing as she fell. Falling straight toward the rocks below.

"Wren!"

The Kantos lifted the helian container, taunting him.

Wren or the helian.

Malax didn't stop to think. He took two huge steps and dived off the cliff. He arrowed straight down, toward where Wren was flailing in the air. He hit her, wrapping his body around her.

Then he commanded his helian, and a burst of power shoved them away from the rocks below.

Seconds later, they hit the water.

CHAPTER FOURTEEN

Wren came up spluttering. She spat out a mouthful of water.

Oh, God. She'd fallen off a fricking cliff. *Damn Kantos.*

"Wren, talk to me."

Malax was holding her and treading water to keep them both afloat. She pushed her sodden hair off her face.

"I'm okay."

Thanks to him. If he hadn't rescued her, she would've hit the rocks for sure. She glanced at the spiky formations and shivered.

Malax ran his hands over her, checking every inch of her. Then he cupped her face, stroking along her cheekbone.

Wren's belly clenched. He'd leaped off a cliff for her. He'd saved her. Again. Apart from her sisters, no one had ever put her first like that.

Then she blinked. "Oh, God, Malax, the helian—"

"We'll find the Kantos." Malax's tone was dark, he started swimming, aiming for the beach. "We will get the helian back."

Suddenly, he stiffened.

"What?" She frowned, looking around the water.

"I sensed something—"

Wren felt the pulse of his helian. It was clearly warning him about something.

At that moment, a giant shadow passed under them in the water. It was *enormous*.

Primal fear made her throat close. "Oh, my God. Beneath us."

"Swim," Malax said grimly.

They both started kicking, aiming for the shore. She tried not to look down. God, that thing could be swimming right at them...

Suddenly, a large tentacle rose up in front of them. She swallowed a scream. It didn't make her think of an octopus. This thing was long, sleek, and armored, and covered with sharp spikes along its length.

Shit.

She moved her arms, kicking harder. They had to get out of the water.

She heard a huge splash behind them, and she saw Malax glance backward.

His jaw tightened. "Keep swimming." He shoved her toward the shore. "Get to the beach." He raised his arm, treading water.

She saw his helian flash and a weapon form on his arm. Some sort of blaster.

Boom.

She watched a pulse of energy come from the blaster. She really, really wanted to understand how that worked.

"Go, Wren! Don't look back." She heard more thrashing and splashing in the water behind them.

She looked back. "Fuck."

Looking at the monster made her gut turn to concrete. It was *huge*.

The aquatic alien creature had risen partway out of the water. Water flowed down the dark sides of its armored shell. It was the size of a starship, with a long, elongated, triangular-shaped head, covered with spiky ridges.

And teeth.

So many teeth.

Malax fired again, then cursed. "I said, *don't* look back."

"You had to know that would make me look."

"Swim, Wren!"

He fired again, and the creature let out a deafening roar. Malax grabbed Wren and started swimming toward the shore.

But she heard the splashing. The creature was coming after them.

She tasted bile, fear like acid in her veins. All of a sudden, something shot through the water. A black substance was changing the water. It looked like ink.

Then, slowly, the water around her began to thicken. She kept kicking, but moving her arms and legs was getting harder and harder. The water surrounding them had turned to gel.

Wren let out a whimper.

"Keep going," Malax said. "I won't let it hurt you."

"I don't want it to hurt you, either!"

The creature let out another roar. God, it was *right* behind them. Malax wrapped an arm around her, and she clung tight. He was still kicking, but they were barely moving.

A splash of water. They both looked back, and watched the creature rise up out of the water. Its huge jaws opened and it rushed toward them.

Boom.

The noise in the sky made her look up. A ship appeared. A second later, laser fire tore into the creature.

It started shrieking and thrashing in the water. More laser blasts hammered into it.

Another piercing screech, and the creature went still, flopping down into the water. It floated for a second, then began to sink slowly.

Malax smiled. "My warriors are here."

Wren eyed the black Eon shuttle as it circled above. *God.* A sob burst out of her chest. "I want *out* of this water."

He pressed a kiss to the side of her head. "Hold on to me, Wren. I'll get you out."

MALAX DRAGGED Wren out of the water and up onto the sand.

Sabin's deep voice came through his communicator. "Malax? Are you hurt?"

"We're fine, Sabin. You have very good timing."

"I'm glad you're okay. We'll find a safe place to land and—"

The line started to crackle.

Then the low sound of a muted boom that Malax knew all too well.

The sound of ships entering the atmosphere made Wren gasp. They both looked up.

Beyond the *Rengard's* sleek shuttle, several Kantos ships had appeared. They were all large cruisers, with several long leg-like protrusions and an armored central hull. They started firing on the shuttle.

"Holy shit," Wren said.

"Sabin? Sabin?" His security commander didn't respond. "The Kantos are jamming comms."

Malax watched the shuttle swing away, moving into defensive maneuvers.

Suddenly, a small Kantos swarm ship whizzed overhead. It had clearly come from one of the larger ships. It was heading toward the ruins.

Cren. It was coming for the helian.

"Come on. They're going after the helian."

"We have to stop them," she said.

Together, they jogged up the hill. Wren's wet hair was plastered to her head, but her face was set with grim determination.

As they ran toward the ruins, Malax felt conflicted. He wanted to stop the Kantos, but he now felt a competing urge...to keep Wren safe.

"There." She pointed.

The archway appeared and they sprinted through it. The cobblestone road was uneven, and dotted with puddles of water. The ruins rose up around them, all made of large blocks of gray stone. Most of the blocks were covered in green moss, and vines twisted between the crumbling buildings.

A structure that looked like a large temple rose in the center of the city. The Kantos swarm ship was hovering above it.

Malax glanced back. His shuttle was still fighting the Kantos cruisers. His jaw tightened. They were heavily outgunned. He hoped the *Rengard* wasn't far away.

He turned back. He couldn't help them right now. All he could do was ensure the Kantos did not get the helian off the planet.

He looked down at Wren. "I need you to hide."

She thrust her hands on her hips. "No, I can help."

Suddenly, two Kantos hunting bugs leaped out of some rubble. The iridescent purple creatures leaped onto some broken pillars, antennae on the tops of their heads waving back and forth.

Cren. If there were bugs on the ground, that meant there was probably a Kantos kill squad close by.

"Stay back." His sword formed on his arm, and he rushed forward. The bugs leaped at him.

Malax spun and whirled. He threw all his strength behind his swings. He skewered one bug, and flung it off his weapon. He turned to find the other bug hanging back warily, as it studied Malax. Its antennae were moving fast, clearly agitated. Suddenly, there was movement out of the corner of his eye.

He sucked in a breath. Two more hunting bugs were

slinking out of the shadows. One branched off, heading toward Wren.

By Eschar's arrow. Malax morphed a smaller knife from his helian, grabbed it, and looked back at Wren.

"Here."

He tossed the knife, and it landed blade down near her feet. She darted forward and picked it up. She swallowed and raised the blade. Her face was filled with fear, but she didn't let it stop her from turning to face the bug.

The first bug leaped at Malax. He lifted his arm. Throwing stars shot from his helian. They sliced into the creature. It made a terrible noise, skittering backward into the rubble.

He spun to see another bug diving at him. He slashed out with his sword.

Seconds later, it was down, bleeding on the paved ground.

He spun and saw the final bug was attacking Wren. It darted at her.

She slashed at it with her knife. "I'm *so* over freaking Kantos."

The bug skittered back.

"Wren? Do you require assistance?" Sassy's voice rang out over the fight.

"Not right now, Sassy." Wren lunged again with her knife.

"My scans detected a strange energy signature in your vicinity," Sassy continued.

"Shh, Sassy!"

Malax fought a smile and fired a throwing star at the

bug. It sliced off an antenna and lodged in the creature's head.

"How do you like that?" Wren cried.

He openly smiled now. His bloodthirsty woman. But his smile dissolved as he looked past Wren.

The Kantos kill squad had arrived.

There were six soldiers, and beside them, the elite who'd stolen the helian. It still clutched the container under one arm.

"Wren, I'm detecting several Kantos soldiers," Sassy said.

"Not now, Sassy!"

Malax dragged in a deep breath. He needed to keep the Kantos engaged and away from Wren. "Get out of here, Wren!"

He took two steps and broke into a run. He leaped up onto a pillar and then onto a higher one. He could hear the soldiers buzzing, all of them shifting to follow him. He leaped over the top of them, raising his sword above his head. He came down in the center of them, crashing his weapon down into the closest soldier.

Malax knew there were too many of them. The best Eon warrior couldn't hope to beat an entire kill squad.

But he wanted to give Wren a chance. He prayed that for once, she listened to his orders.

A sharp Kantos arm sliced through his armor. He hissed, feeling blood seeping down his gut. Ignoring the pain, he thrust his sword at another one.

Another soldier smashed a blow into his lower back, and a tearing pain ripped through him. Gritting his teeth, he swung again. But the swing was clumsy and he missed.

Malax kept fighting, his focus narrowed down onto the fight.

He heard a beep and glanced over. His blood ran cold. Wren was crouched behind a pile of rubble, swiping furiously on her tablet. "Wren! Go."

"No way." Her tone was bad-tempered. "Give me a second."

Several soldiers turned and looked in her direction. Malax's gut tightened. He was running out of options.

Another soldier rushed at him and he braced.

Then Wren lifted her head and smiled.

Bright lights flared all around them. Malax narrowed his eyes. The light was coming out of the ruins.

What the cren?

CHAPTER FIFTEEN

She'd done it!

"Nice work, Sassy." Wren clutched her tablet, watching as the alien technology still active in the ruins flared to life around them. A hum of energy filled the air.

"It was lucky my scans picked up the alien energy signature," Sassy said. "Once, this city possessed an advanced security system."

In front of Wren, colored lights flared. A wall of laser beams rose up, cutting through several of the Kantos soldiers.

"Badass." Wren grinned.

"Uh-oh."

She frowned at Sassy's words. "What?"

"This system is too complex," Sassy said. "There is too much data, and it's overwhelming my system."

"Just focus the weapons fire on the Kantos."

Wren watched as more laser fire took another Kantos

down. The remaining soldiers were diving for cover, long legs flailing.

But lasers were firing all over the place now. It looked like the world's craziest light show. Wren bit her lip and ducked. Crap, it was totally out of control.

A laser blast hit the stone wall above her head, and she dived for the ground. *Shittity, shit, shit.* There was a hot burn on her skin and rubble collapsed behind her.

"Wren!" Malax jumped over a block of stone and slid in next to her.

"I accessed the ancient city's defense system." She gripped the tablet harder, trying desperately to shut the system down. "But it's out of control."

Suddenly, a mechanical whirr filled the air. Nearby, the stone floor opened up, and a large weapon rose out of the ground. It swiveled, aiming into the sky.

"Uh-oh," Wren murmured.

The weapon fired. Several pulses of green laser speared into the sky.

Malax cursed. "It's firing on the ships."

She watched as one Kantos ship was hit. *Ka-boom.* The explosion filled the sky like fireworks, and she threw up her arm to shield her eyes. The ship broke up and plummeted toward the sea.

The weapons system continued to fire.

Laser fire hit the rock wall above their heads again, and she and Malax ducked down. Chunks of rock rained down on them. He shifted his body to cover hers.

When Wren looked up again, she realized the weapons system was firing on both the *Rengard*'s shuttle and the remaining Kantos ship.

Shit.

"Can you turn it off?" Malax bit out.

She swiped the screen. "I'm trying."

More lasers cut through rock nearby, and she heard a rumble.

"Malax!"

Above them, a large pillar started to topple.

Malax scooped her up and ran. He leaped over a low stone wall and they landed...just as the pillar hit the ground. Rocks and dust filled the air.

She lifted her head, coughing. Through the dust, she couldn't see any Kantos. Fingers crossed that meant they were all dead. But what about the helian?

More lasers flared to life, like a grid of light, cutting everywhere in a deadly light show.

"Overload warning," Sassy said, her voice strangely monotone.

"Sassy, I need your help to switch this off—"

"Overload—" Sassy's screen blinked off.

"No. No." Wren tried to coax her tablet back to life. *Nothing.*

She looked up and saw that the *Rengard's* shuttle was trying to evade the laser fire. She looked back at Malax, horrified.

"I can't control it."

He gripped her arms. "Wren—"

She shook her head. "I can't get into the system and shut it off. This is what I'm supposed to be good at."

Malax rose, bringing her with him. "Wren, you gave us a chance, now we need to get out of here."

Laser fire arrowed in their direction. He dived on her,

pressing her to the ground. As larger rocks rained down on them, Wren choked back a scream.

"Come on." He urged her up. Bent over almost double, they ran along the wall of the closest building.

Then Malax picked her up like a football and ran full-out. He pounded up a set of broken steps, dodging through some overgrown vines.

He was headed for the temple. No laser fire seemed to be touching it.

Wren glanced back, and spotted two Kantos soldiers following them. The aliens were busy dodging the laser fire as well.

Then Malax ran into the temple and they were plunged into darkness.

MALAX SET Wren down inside the temple. The building was mostly intact, and he looked around the shadows. It was covered in stone carvings and ornate walls. Or what was left of them.

"Are you sure you can't turn off the ancient weapons systems?" he asked.

Wren looked up at him and winced. "I can't. It isn't responding."

He heard noises and pulled her deeper into the shadows. He heard the buzz of Kantos and guessed the remaining Kantos soldiers were taking shelter in here, too. Grimly, he pulled her deeper into the temple.

"I saw two soldiers," she whispered.

He nodded. Here the shadows weren't as deep. Some

of the stonework gave off a golden glow. At least they could see where they were going. He pushed some vines aside and kept moving.

Suddenly, Malax felt the tile beneath his foot depress. *Click.* The sound of a grinding mechanism echoed through the room.

Projectiles shot out from the far wall. Right at them.

Malax dropped, dragging Wren to the floor. He pressed her flat, covering her body with his. The spear-like projectiles whizzed over their heads, slamming into the opposite wall.

"Oh, God," Wren said.

Moments later, the weapons stopped. Carefully, Malax and Wren sat up.

Cren. The temple must be riddled with traps.

"Come on." He pulled her up. "Watch where you step."

She made a noise. "What am I watching for?"

"I have no idea."

"*Not* helpful, warrior."

They continued onward, moving cautiously. But they hadn't gone much farther when a rumbling vibration started beneath their feet. Ribbons of dust fell from the ceiling.

The floor split open, a chasm opening up directly in front of them.

"Jump!" he yelled.

"I can't. It's too far."

Malax lifted Wren into his arms and leaped over the widening gap.

She looked back, shaking the dust off her hair. "I have a really bad feeling about this."

They continued carefully down the dark tunnel, and stepped into a large, round room. A domed roof rose up, disappearing into darkness overhead. The remnants of crumbling statues lined the walls. They were all imposing humanoids, with large bodies and flat faces.

The noise of something scraping on rock caught their ears. They both froze in place, searching the shadows.

The Kantos elite stepped into view, clutching the helian container. It stared at them, eyes bright in the dim light.

You can't stop us.

"Yes, I can." Malax held his arm out, his sword forming.

The Kantos retreated a few scuttling steps backward, then yanked something out of its armor. He tossed it into the air with his clawed hand.

"Watch out," Wren yelled.

The small, scaled ball sailed into the air. Malax was already diving toward Wren when the object burst open. Black spikes burst out of the Kantos weapon. They sailed through the air, racing toward them.

He shoved Wren out of the way, and three projectiles slammed into his shoulder and arm, piercing his armor. Sharp pain tore through him.

"Malax!"

Gritting his teeth, he sucked in a breath. He staggered, dropping to his knees. He had to stay conscious. He had to protect Wren.

She ran toward him, dropping down beside him. She

cupped his cheek, her horrified gaze on the ugly, black spikes protruding from his armor.

Behind her, he saw the Kantos loom closer, raising another round, scaled ball.

She was right in the line of fire.

The Kantos threw the weapon.

No. Malax threw his arm out, reaching for her.

The Kantos weapon exploded, and it felt like time slowed down. The spikes powered through the air, Wren turned her head, mouth opening in a scream.

Not enough time to toss her out of the way.

Suddenly, black scales flowed off his armor. They streamed off him, flying through the air. The scales hit Wren and she jolted. They flowed over her body.

Shock and awe arrowed into his gut. As he watched his helian protect Wren, a sense of rightness flowed through him.

A second later, she was covered in scaled armor. The first projectile skimmed her and she was already moving, aided by the helian armor. She bent backward and another projectile flew past her, the next one glanced off her arm but didn't pierce the armor.

She leaped into the air, somersaulting backward. She landed on her feet, looking shocked.

The Kantos elite stared at them for a second, then turned, and ran deeper into the temple.

Cren. Malax forced himself to block out his pain and pushed to his feet. He gripped the spike lodged in his chest, pulled it out, and tossed it. He yanked the other two out of his arm, dropping them on the tiles.

"Malax, you're bleeding." Wren's voice was clogged with emotion.

"My helian will slow it and start healing me. We have to get that other helian back."

She nodded. "Thanks for the armor."

He cupped her cheek. "I want you to stay safe." He wouldn't tell her yet of the significance of his helian bonding with her. Now wasn't the time.

He charged after the Kantos, quickly spotting the elite at the far side of the expanse. It was searching for a way out.

Malax tackled the alien and they skidded across the floor. The elite's sharp legs kicked and flailed, but Malax gritted his teeth and pinned it down to the tiles.

They wrestled, both fighting to gain the upper hand.

Malax could feel the blood seeping out of his wounds. Every jolt bumped them, and his strength was draining out of him. The Kantos sensed it.

The elite's eyes flashed.

I will kill you, Eon. And I will kill your Terran, as well.

Anger surged through Malax, but the Kantos got one arm free, lifting the sharp edge high.

Suddenly, a glowing, gold sword slammed down, piercing through the elite's chest.

The Kantos bucked, eyes flaring.

Malax looked up.

Wren. She drove the sword attached to her arm down, her face strained as she worked the blade through the Kantos' hard shell.

The elite slumped, releasing the container with the helian. The glass container hit the floor, and broke, the small, slug-like helian rolling out onto the tiles.

CHAPTER SIXTEEN

W ren yanked the sword back, and stood there, heaving in air.

She was a *badass*.

She raised her arm, her armor and sword glowing faintly in the shadows. This *rocked*.

Malax surged up, and kicked the Kantos elite's body, checking that it was dead.

Wren turned and saw the helian on the ground. She quickly scooped the small creature up and stuck it in a pocket on her belt.

"Are you okay?" she asked him. The bleeding on his arm and shoulder seemed to have stopped.

He nodded, eyeing her armor. "Yes, we need—"

There was the sound of running footsteps and they both spun. Two more Kantos ran into the room.

Oh, no.

Malax lifted his arm and she watched as his sword morphed into a blaster weapon. He fired on the aliens.

The blasts lit up the dim space.

As she watched, several ugly bugs skidded in behind the Kantos soldiers.

Really not good. The familiar, humming buzz of communication filled the air. The bugs charged forward like hunting dogs.

Shit. Wren scrambled back, as Malax took several steps backward. Her boot caught on something and she tripped, landing on her ass. She scrambled back, and suddenly saw one of the bugs bounding toward her. She glanced quickly over at Malax.

Two bugs and the soldiers were targeting him. He'd morphed his blaster back into a sword, and, as the first bug reached him, he slashed out with skill and precision.

Wren glanced back, just as the other bug headed her way. It jumped into the air. *Oh, God.* Heart pounding, she threw her arm up.

All of a sudden, throwing stars shot out of her armor. They sliced into the Kantos bug. With a screech, it hit the tiled floor. Its six legs spread out, scrambling as it tried to stand, but clearly, tendons were severed.

Wren looked at her scales on her arm where the throwing stars had come from. *Wow.*

A second Kantos bug came out of nowhere, slinking forward. It had a hard, striped shell, and huge, snapping mandibles. It made a hissing noise.

Wren managed to get to her feet, just as the creature rushed at her, attacking with a snap of its mandibles. In her head, she imagined a huge can of bug spray, but unfortunately, her new armor couldn't seem to create that. She dodged, but a sharp leg hit her and she felt the rake of it through the armor on her arm.

The hot sting made her wince. *Ow.*

She moved backward and saw a row of carved blocks. She leaped onto one, running along them. Turning, she aimed at the bug hunting her.

Throwing stars. Throwing stars. As soon as she thought it, they morphed on her wrist and shot out at the bug.

The bug jolted and let out a wild hiss.

Take that. Wren spun and almost lost her balance. She threw out her arms, and her armor helped center her.

Cool. Eon armor was the cure for clumsiness.

She kept running along the blocks. She heard another hiss and watched the bug jump up on the block behind her. It leaped closer, its yellow eyes on her.

Okay, what next? She needed to take this bug down. She patted the pocket on her belt and felt the helian move. It was safe.

Wren leaped onto another block, but saw the bug was gaining. She imagined the sword on her arm again. Suddenly, it formed once more, just as it had earlier.

Oh, wow. Thankfully, Eve and Lara had forced Wren to train with them on occasion. They'd wanted her to know the basics of fighting so she could protect herself. She wasn't a swordswoman by any means, but she wasn't completely clueless, either.

She heard a grunt and a crash. Across the room, she saw Malax was pinned down by a Kantos soldier and another bug.

Her heart stopped.

She watched as the Kantos soldier raised his arm and then stabbed down.

No! Her body locked. "Malax!"

He wrenched free at the last second and rolled. The Kantos' arm pierced Malax's shoulder, instead of his chest.

Bile rose in her mouth. She had to help him.

Her bug launched itself in her direction, and fury flooded her. She was so fucking sick of everyone pushing her around—Lance, the Space Corps, the Kantos. She swung her arm and shouted. Her sword slashed the bug's softer underbelly. Green blood sprayed, and the bug crashed to the floor. But Wren didn't stay to watch. She leaped off the stone block, running toward Malax.

"Sassy! God, please be back online!"

"I'm here."

Thank God. "We need to help Malax." As she watched, the Kantos slammed his other arm down, pinning Malax through his other shoulder. Malax was bleeding, but still fighting. He was heaving against his captors, even as blood flowed on the floor.

"I can use the alien technology again," Sassy said.

Shit. The crazy alien weapons were just as likely to hurt Malax. But she was still too far away, and if she didn't do something, he was going to die.

She watched the Kantos bug getting closer, mandibles snapping, readying to tear out Malax's throat.

"Do it," Wren cried.

"Initializing."

A sharp whistling sound went through the room and the floor started to vibrate. Bright light speared down from the roof, and Wren swallowed a scream. As she watched, every single Kantos in the room was turned to stone. Even the ones standing over Malax.

She gasped, staring in horror.

A second later, the frozen Kantos vaporized, their bodies turning to dust.

Oh. My. God.

Malax sat up, his eyes wide with disbelief. Wren spun, scanning the entire space. All the Kantos were gone.

"Sassy?" She was too afraid to move, in case she got incinerated.

"I've shut the system off."

Gingerly, Wren started toward Malax. "Are you okay?" God, his armor was slick with blood, and torn in places.

He nodded. "My helian is attempting to slow the bleeding and heal my wounds."

She smiled at him and he smiled back.

Just then, a slab of rock slammed down from the roof, smashing into the ground nearby. Wren screamed and staggered back. *Shit.* Dust filled the air and she coughed.

Another stone slammed down, and another.

"The building's integrity has been compromised," Sassy said. "Get out."

Wren looked at Malax. He was up on his knees, staring at her.

"We have to go," she shouted.

He nodded and started to rise...just as the roof collapsed.

Right on top of him.

Shock and fear ripped into Wren like a wild animal. She couldn't breathe. More rocks fell and the air filled with dust. Coughing, she threw her arm up to deflect a few smaller rocks. They bounced off her.

She lifted her head, and felt as though the ground had dropped away from beneath her.

No. Where Malax had been, there was now just a massive pile of rubble and boulders.

Agony split her chest open. "No. Malax!"

Wren dropped to her knees beside the rocks and started clawing at them.

MALAX COUGHED HARD. The air around him was choked with dust.

He heaved in a breath, working through the pain. He waved a hand to clear the air. His helian glowed, giving just enough light for him to see that a large stone beam was resting above him, holding the rest of the rubble off him. He was trapped in a small space.

He shifted, pain shooting through his shoulders. He probed the wounds carefully. His helian had already stopped the bleeding. They weren't life-threatening.

Above him, he heard a noise—Wren's frantic cries.

Grimly, Malax gripped the rocks above him and started pushing his way through.

Wren's sobbing ripped at him. He heard her sorrow and terror. He kept pushing rocks out of the way, and finally punched through the last of the rubble.

"Malax!" She stared at him for a beat, then reached for him.

Her face was covered in dust, and tears tracked down her cheeks. When her hands touched him, like she was assuring herself that he was real, her face crumpled and she started crying.

He pulled her close, crushing her to his chest.

"I thought... I thought..." Her voice broke.

He held her tight, stroking her dusty hair. "I'm all right."

"I thought you were dead."

"I'm right here."

"The rocks." She lifted her head, gently touching the rips in his armor. "And you're hurt."

"A few scratches."

Her eyes widened. "The Kantos skewered right through your shoulder and arm!"

"My helian has already stopped the bleeding. The wounds are healing." He didn't tell her that despite his symbiont dulling the pain, it still hurt like being dipped in the fire sprays of Jad.

Malax pulled Wren up on her toes and kissed her. He meant for it to be quick, but as soon as he tasted her, and heard her sigh, he groaned. He deepened it, kissing her like their lives depended on it.

It was over too soon, but he sensed her body relax a little.

"Let's get out of here," he said.

She nodded and he scooped her into his arms.

"You shouldn't carry me, you're hurt—"

"I'm fine. Remember, a war commander never lies."

With a sigh, she pressed her cheek gently against his chest. Turning, he made his way out of the temple, keeping a close eye out for any more traps.

When they stepped outside, the sounds of combat filled the air. The sky was filled with more ships: both Kantos and Eon. The battling ships filled the sky with laser fire, smoke, and explosions. Fighters from the *Rengard* were engaging swarms of small Kantos ships.

Wren looked up. "Oh, God."

Malax's communicator flared to life. "Malax?"

It was Sabin.

"We're here, Sabin. We're at the alien temple in the center of the city."

"I'm aboard a fighter. We're coming to get you."

A second later, a sleek Eon fighter swept overhead. The blue lights along its sides glowed brightly. There was a burst of air around them and Wren tucked her face into his neck.

The fighter landed in front of the temple, and the door opened at the back.

Malax jogged down the steps and over to the ship. Sabin met them in the doorway.

His security commander looked relieved to see him. The faint purple in the man's eyes flared.

"Thank the warriors." Sabin's gaze fell to Wren. "You're both okay?"

"Minor injuries." Malax strode aboard the ship.

Wren snorted. "The war commander's idea of minor differs from mine."

Sabin closed the door and called out to the pilots. Malax moved to the small seats at the back, that folded out from the wall. A second later, the ship shot back into the sky.

"The helian?" Sabin asked.

Malax frowned. "We lost it in the—"

"I have it." Wren pulled something from her belt.

Malax blinked. A small helian was resting on her palm. A laugh broke from his chest. "You have it."

She nodded. When Sabin came forward, holding a helian container, she held her palm over the top of it. For a second, the helian clung to her, then slipped into the jar.

"Bye, little guy," she murmured.

Sabin looked amused. "You realize that 'little guy' is an ancient, sentient, and powerful alien being."

She shrugged, leaning back in Malax's arms. "It's still little."

As he sat, Sabin's gaze moved over Wren again. The man's gaze flicked up to Malax's. "She wears your armor."

Malax nodded. Wren was his mate. He'd suspected it, already wanted it, but the way his helian responded to her confirmed it.

Wren was his—now and forever. His to cherish, protect, and love.

"I know, isn't it cool?" Then Wren's smile faded, as she eyed both men. Her gaze moved from Malax to Sabin and back again. "What am I missing? Why do you guys look so serious?"

"It's nothing," Malax nuzzled her hair. "We'll talk later. Right now, we need to get back to the *Rengard*." *Alive.*

The Eon fighter continued climbing into the sky.

"Swarm ships incoming," the co-pilot yelled.

Malax saw the swarm ships rushing at them. He set Wren beside him and pulled the harness over her, then fastened his own. Just in time, because seconds later, they were both tossed against the straps.

The Eon pilots worked together, their ship diving and rolling, to avoid the enemy fighters.

But the farther they flew, the more the number of ships in the sky intensified. Swarm ships sped past, Eon fighters pursuing. Laser traces lit up the sky.

Wren's hand flashed out and grabbed his. He squeezed her fingers.

"Brace," the pilot yelled.

A blast hit their ship. Wren gasped and the ship vibrated. The two warriors in the cockpit stayed focused. Malax kept his emotions under control. He had to show his complete confidence in his warriors.

Eon fighters were battling some larger Kantos battle-cruisers. Missiles flew, fast and hard, exploding in the sky.

Then, he spied the familiar shape of the *Rengard*. It was in orbit, and under heavy attack from several Kantos ships.

He sucked in a breath. So many. His warship was heavily outnumbered.

Frowning, he looked at Sabin. "Reinforcements?"

Sabin looked grim. "The *Desteron* and the *Vymerion* are inbound."

"But they're too far away," Malax said.

Sabin nodded.

So, there would be no help. Malax stared out at the

fight outside, turning options over in his head. "We will fight until the others arrive."

It was what warriors did. They fought and protected.

Just as his warriors had on Dalath Prime. Despite the odds, his warriors had been heroes that day.

More swarm ships crowded the sky, and a new squadron of fighters poured out of the *Rengard*, arrowing into fight formation. Seconds later, laser fire lit up the sky. He watched several ships explode—both Kantos and Eon.

His gut heavy, Malax closed his eyes for a moment. He was losing warriors, and the pain was immense. They were his people to protect.

He felt Wren squeeze his fingers. "I'm so sorry, Malax."

He nodded. Just that small touch helped and he opened his eyes.

"Hold on!" The pilot called out. "We have several swarm ships chasing us."

A blast hit them, and the ship shuddered.

Another blast tossed them all sideways, and flames flickered over the outside of the ship, covering the viewscreen.

"Shields holding," the co-pilot said, voice tense. "For now."

Malax gripped the armrests of his seat. They needed to reach the *Rengard,* or they were dead.

CHAPTER SEVENTEEN

The ship was hit again, and the wild jolt had Wren gritting her teeth.

The warriors in the pilot seats were shouting, and beside her Malax looked grim.

"Get us through that gap," the pilot yelled.

"More swarm ships incoming." The co-pilot's voice vibrated with tension.

The ship picked up speed, diving and rolling. Wren gripped onto Malax. They pulled up so sharply that her stomach dropped then lodged in her throat. Oh, God, she hoped she wasn't going to puke.

She stared at the hard lines of Malax's face. He stared out the viewscreen, watching his fighters. She'd seen some get destroyed and knew it was painful for him. She felt the tension throb off him.

A massive explosion rocked the ship.

"Missile," the co-pilot yelled. "We're hit!"

"*Cren*," the pilot shouted. "We're losing shields. War Commander, we aren't going to make it."

"Keep flying, Naton." Malax's voice was firm, commanding, no hint of panic. He touched his communicator. "*Rengard?*"

"Malax." It was Airen's harried voice. "We're under heavy attack and losing our shields."

Malax cursed, staring at the floor.

The fighter was hit again, shuddering hard.

"We've lost an engine," the co-pilot called out.

Wren shook her head. She was not going to die here! She didn't want to explode into tiny pieces, or get sucked out into space. She wasn't going to lose Malax.

She undid the straps of her harness.

Malax's head whipped around. "Wren—"

Ignoring him, she darted forward. She moved between the two pilots' chairs, gripping one to keep her balance. Another jolt almost sent her crashing to the floor.

The pilots looked up at her, faces lined with strain. She slammed her hand with her blue wristband against the console.

"Sassy." The band on her wrist flared and she felt Sassy linking with the ship's controls. "We have work to do."

Malax's big body pressed against her back. "Get back in your seat."

"I can help," she said.

Malax growled.

She turned her head to look at him. "I can fight, too. In my own way."

"You don't belong up here," he bit out.

The words were a slash to her heart. For a second, it was Lance's voice echoing in her head. *Screw that.* She lifted her chin. "Do you really believe that?" She paused and swallowed. "Don't break my heart, Malax."

He cursed, looking torn. "Wren...I just want to protect you."

"And I want to protect you, too. Let me do what I'm good at."

He stared at her for what felt like forever. Then he nodded. "Silan, move."

The co-pilot shifted out of his seat. Wren dropped into it.

"Sassy, we're taking control."

"Nice," Sassy replied. "This is a very nice ship."

Wren felt a jolt run through her body. She stayed perched on the edge of the seat, leaning forward. The fight outside made her gut roll, but she stayed focused.

They had to get to the *Rengard*. That was her only goal.

The band on her wrist glowed brighter and got warm. Soon, it was so hot that it was almost burning.

"Let's go," she said.

She kept her shoulders back, staring straight ahead. She sucked in a breath. She could *feel* the ship—all its systems, the damage, the weapons, the flight controls. It felt like a thousand thoughts were racing through her brain.

Staring at the *Rengard*, she and Sassy charted their path to the warship. The fighter shot forward.

Oh, God, she was flying an Eon fighter.

Faster than she could if she had to tap the controls, she flew them through a gap between several Kantos ships. They picked up speed.

"Watch out!" the pilot yelled.

She calmly looked at the swarm ships. The fighter tipped, zooming through a narrow gap and dodging the laser fire.

She felt Malax's hands clamp onto her, holding her in place.

"How is she doing this?" the pilot breathed.

She ignored the warrior, focused on flying. Ahead, a large Kantos ship started to break apart.

Aiming for the wreckage, they moved even faster. There was only a narrow gap, and lots of debris.

"*Cren*, we're going to hit it," Sabin said.

Adrenaline and excitement charged through Wren. She felt like a goddess, power at her fingertips, in full control.

They shot through the narrow gap, with just inches to spare on either side.

Diving, she dodged debris from the ship. When she pulled them up, the *Rengard* filled the viewscreen.

The warriors in her fighter cheered.

Malax's mouth pressed to her ear. "You are amazing."

More Kantos swarm ships came at them and she returned fire. One exploded and the others dodged away.

Now, to get aboard the *Rengard*. But as they watched, she saw the huge Kantos cruisers bombarding the warship with fire.

Wren bit her lip. Surely, they couldn't hold up under the sustained barrage for long.

"We need to approach from the rear," Malax said.

She nodded. She switched course, their fighter zooming toward the back of the warship. As they got closer, she saw the *Rengard* was damaged in several places. One gaping hole exposed several decks.

"Oh, God," she murmured.

"There are shields in place to protect the breaches." Malax's voice was a harsh rasp.

But as they raced toward the *Rengard*'s docking bay, Wren knew in her heart that they were losing the fight.

MALAX HEARD the clank as their fighter touched down in the *Rengard's* rear docking bay. A second later, the rear door opened.

Wren pulled her hand back and rose. She wobbled and he grabbed her arm.

"Wren?"

"Just a bit dizzy."

"You saved our lives," the pilot said. "Without you, we would be dead."

"Thank you," the co-pilot said with a nod.

Her face pale, she managed a small smile. Malax frowned, keeping an eye on her. She was off balance.

"You were incredible, Wren," he said quietly.

"Thanks."

He kept his hand on her arm as they exited the ship. A small group of warriors were waiting for them.

"Second Commander Kann-Felis requested you on the bridge," one warrior said.

Malax nodded at them. "Let's go."

Still holding Wren, and with Sabin on his other side, they headed through the corridors. As soon as he stepped onto the bridge, he got a close-up view of the fight on the viewscreen.

His gut hardened. There were Kantos ships everywhere.

"Update on the *Desteron* and the *Vymerion?*" he asked.

Airen spun. She stood in the center of the bridge, commanding the offense. "Glad to see you, Malax, and you Wren." Her flat gaze met Malax's. "The warships are still forty-five ship minutes out."

He cursed. The *Rengard* wouldn't last that long.

Wren gripped his hand, her fingers clenched on his. Her face was still pale, and patches of dust still coated her skin and hair.

Emotions stormed through him, amplified by his helian. She was *his*. His mate. His courageous little Terran.

And he refused to let her die today.

He'd failed his warriors on Dalath Prime, but he wouldn't fail his warriors today or his mate.

"Update me," he ordered Airen.

His second ran through their attack plan and the damage report.

"Reroute power to the forward array," he said.

Airen waved a hand at some warriors, who bent over their consoles.

"You've done excellent work, Airen."

"We're losing," his second said.

Malax glanced at Wren. "I've learned some valuable lessons, Airen." He focused on his second. "We do our best, we don't give up, and when we get knocked down, we get back up."

Airen straightened her shoulders. "Good advice, War Commander."

"Let's keep fighting."

Suddenly, the *Rengard* was hit by a plasma blast. Warriors staggered and fell, and Malax caught Wren, pulling her close.

Nearby, a console exploded. Shouts broke out and warriors ran to extinguish the flames.

"There's an energy overload," a warrior cried.

"It's running through all the systems. We have a cascade."

Malax heard the cries of his warriors, and despite his words to Airen, he knew they were running out of options.

"We have injuries," someone else called out.

Malax straightened. "Call medical. Get Thane and his team here. *Now*. Sabin, get that fire out. Airen, stay focused on our defense. Return fire."

"Some weapons are damaged, Malax," his second said quietly. "But we'll keep fighting."

He continued to bark out orders. Thane arrived with his medical team, pulling the injured warriors to the side to treat them.

Then Malax felt Wren move away. She walked to the nearest console.

"Wren?"

"Let me help."

On the fighter, when she'd spiked in, she'd done things he could barely comprehend. She was the only reason they'd made it back to the *Rengard*. "Do whatever you can."

He watched the blue band glow on her wrist as she plugged into the console.

"Sassy?"

"Initializing," the helian intelligence replied.

He saw Wren's body jolt like she'd been hit by an electric shock. She threw her arms out, her muscles straining.

He moved closer. "Wren?"

"*Rengard*...is a lot bigger than a fighter." She talked through gritted teeth.

"I lost control of the weapons system," a warrior called out, panicked.

"I have it." Wren's voice smoothed into a monotone.

Frowning, Malax moved to stand with her. When her gaze drifted to his, he saw her eyes were glowing bright blue, and making rapid movements.

Suddenly, the *Rengard's* weapons fired. Everything at once—missiles, plasma charges, laser fire.

One large Kantos ship exploded.

The *Rengard* started moving forward.

"She's flying the ship, as well," Airen breathed. "She is doing it all."

"Sassy," Wren said. "Calculate our best attack vectors."

"Calculating."

Malax saw the shock on the faces of his warriors, but

he knew that Wren and Sassy working together could create miracles.

Wren simply stared ahead. The *Rengard's* weapons fired again. Missiles zoomed across the viewscreen.

The warship picked up speed, going faster than he thought possible at thruster speed. Somehow, with Sassy's help, Wren was pulling extra power and speed from his ship.

A cloud of Kantos swarm ships raced toward them.

"Sassy," Wren murmured.

"I see them."

A squadron of Eon fighters came into view, racing to intercept.

"War Commander." The shocked face of the squadron leader flashed onto the screen. "We've lost control of our fighters. We're still flying, but we aren't in control."

"It's okay, Orin," Malax said. "Sit tight. We have control."

He hoped Wren had control. How she could command the entire *Rengard*, and take control of all his fighters at the same time, he couldn't fathom. He watched the fighters move into formation.

They hit the swarm, flying fast and hard. They flew in dizzying formations, firing on the enemy ships. Soon, the swarm was decimated, and not a single Eon fighter had been hit.

Everyone on the bridge clapped and cheered.

But Malax kept his eyes on Wren.

Her skin was starting to give off a faint blue-white glow. With his enhanced senses, he detected her elevated pulse rate, breathing, and perspiration. Her heart was beating fast. Too fast.

"This is incredible," Airen murmured.

"She and Sassy are working together, and Sassy has her plugged into the ship's controls." He frowned. "But her heart rate is still increasing."

Now he saw Wren's eyelids fluttering fast. Unnaturally fast.

"Malax." His doctor appeared by his side. "Her vitals..."

"I know."

"She can't keep this up much longer," Thane warned.

Malax stared up at the screen. There were still too many Kantos ships for them to handle. Wren was giving them a chance to survive. If he pulled her out now, they were still unlikely to last until their backup arrived.

And if he left her plugged in...

He felt the terrible decision settle on his shoulders. Risk Wren's life, to save his warriors. Or pull her out, risk his warriors, and hope that they could keep the Kantos at bay until the *Desteron* or the *Vymerion* arrived.

Wren pulled in a shuddering breath. He saw foam at the corner of her mouth.

Enough. His warriors were trained for war, Wren wasn't trained for this.

He gripped her shoulders. "Wren, let go."

"No... Not finished." He heard the pain vibrating through her voice.

"Malax, you need to get her out now," Thane said urgently.

"*Now*, Wren," Malax barked.

"No—"

He saw a trickle of blood come from her nose.

"You're killing yourself." He pulled her flush against him. "I can't lose you. I love you."

Her face lifted, and she let out a shocked gasp. He saw the glow in her eyes dim. Then suddenly, she was released from the system.

Thank the warriors.

She collapsed into his arms.

And that's when Malax realized her heart wasn't beating. "Wren? Wren?" He laid her flat on the floor. Panic was an ugly burn in his throat. "Thane, help her!"

CHAPTER EIGHTEEN

Wren came to flat on her back on the floor of the bridge. The doctor and Malax were leaning over her.

Malax's eyes were closed and he looked destroyed.

"Who died?" she asked.

His eyes snapped open. "Wren?"

She tried to sit up and started coughing. Everything in her body hurt.

"Thank the warriors." Malax pulled her into his arms, rocking her, and holding her close. He pressed his face to her hair.

"I'm okay." God, her voice sounded weak and scratchy.

"Your heart stopped."

"What?" She gripped him and looked into his face. She saw the nightmare still in his eyes and realized she'd scared her warrior. "I'm all right."

He nodded and gently touched his lips to hers.

"I thought I heard you say—" She broke off.

"I love you," he said.

Her heart knocked against her ribs. "That's what I thought you said." Malax *loved* her. Emotion flooded her.

Then the noise around her registered. Voices were shouting and Airen was giving orders.

"Did we beat the Kantos?" Wren tried to see over his shoulder.

He shifted and she saw the fight was still raging. An Eon fighter exploded, and a Kantos cruiser moved closer to the *Rengard*.

Wren felt fear settle into her gut like a rock.

"You gave us a chance," Malax said. "You were incredible."

But it hadn't been enough. Her fingers tightened on him.

"Malax," Airen cried. "We've lost engines. We can't move. We have Kantos bugs eating into the hull."

God, they were sitting ducks. Wren tried to swallow down her panic. "I'll plug-in again."

Malax growled. "You are *not* going to kill yourself."

Thane nodded. "It will kill you."

Malax rose, holding her close. "Concentrate fire on the main Kantos battlecruiser." He set her on her feet, eyeing her to make sure she was steady.

She locked her knees. Then she watched him give orders, his voice firm but calm. His warriors responded, the tension on the bridge lowering. His warriors snapped back to attention, focusing on their jobs.

That was her war commander. Doing what he was

born to do, and being pretty darn amazing. Her warrior would fight. He'd protect his people to his dying breath.

And he'd protect her. He was hers, and he made her feel safer than she'd ever felt. This amazing warrior loved her just as she was, and she loved him back.

She moved to his side. "Sassy, can you help with repairs?"

"Yes," the intelligence answered. "I'm running diagnostics now."

They might not survive the battle. Bittersweet pain rushed through Wren. She was in love, and she wanted more time with Malax. She wanted to see her sisters again.

A heavy blast hit the *Rengard*. The ship shuddered and she slammed into Malax.

He pulled her close. "Wren." His voice was harsh.

"We don't give up," she told him. "Ever."

His hand slid into her hair, his gaze locked on hers.

"War Commander," a warrior called out. "A new Kantos battlecruiser is approaching. It's locking weapons on us."

Wren saw the huge ship looming. It looked like a giant bug, with a bronze-brown hull, and leg-like protrusions from the main hull of the ship. Her stomach dropped away. "Oh God."

"I love you, Wren," Malax said.

She swallowed. "I love you, too."

Suddenly, there was a brilliant burst of light. Wren winced.

Then her eyes went wide. A ship had jumped right in between the *Rengard* and the battlecruiser.

Shocked gasps erupted across the bridge. Wren gripped Malax's arm.

It wasn't the *Desteron* or an Eon warship.

It was a *Terran* ship.

The Terran cruiser was far smaller than the Kantos battlecruiser, but it was bristling with weapons. As they watched, the ship flew straight at the Kantos ship, moving into a hard circle around the battlecruiser.

"It's so fast," Airen said.

The Terran ship circled the Kantos cruiser, so close the cruiser couldn't lock weapons. The Terran ship started firing.

"How is this possible?" Wren said.

Malax shook his head, his gold-black gaze locked on the fight.

"I contacted them," Sassy said. "I detected they were in range, and small enough for me to facilitate a star jump to our location." Sassy sounded awfully smug.

A rain of missiles slammed into the Kantos battle-cruiser, exploding along the enemy's hull.

Wren smiled. "Sassy, you rock."

"I sure do," Sassy agreed.

MALAX WATCHED in shock as the Kantos battlecruiser began to break up.

Despite its size, the Terran ship had helped them beat the Kantos. He watched the smaller ship turn, locking lasers on incoming Kantos ships.

All around him, his warriors cheered.

Wren laughed, tugging on his hand and leaning into his side.

Then alarms blared across the bridge.

Wren's laughter cut off. "What now?"

"There." He pointed at the screen. A throng of swarm ships were heading straight toward the Terran ship. The cheers subsided, tension filling the bridge.

"Oh, no," she whispered.

He squeezed her hand. "Airen, redirect the last of our fighters."

"Yes, Malax."

He watched as mines flowed out of the side of the Terran ship. As the Kantos swarm ships hit the mines, they started exploding.

"Incoming transmission," a warrior from his comms team called out.

A woman's face flickered up onto the bottom corner of the viewscreen. She was wearing a dark-blue Space Corps uniform, and standing on the bridge of the Terran ship. Her hair was the color of sunshine, and pulled back from the strong features of her face. She had vivid green eyes.

"I'm Captain Allie Borden of the Space Corps ship, *Divergent*."

"War Commander Malax Dann-Jad, of the Eon warship *Rengard*. It's very good to see you, Captain."

The woman nodded. Behind her, the *Divergent*'s bridge hummed with activity as the captain's team worked hard to fight the Kantos.

"We'll keep the Kantos off you for as long as we can, hopefully your incoming reinforcements arrive soon."

Captain Borden's gaze landed on Wren, and her eyes widened a fraction.

Wren gave a small wave. "I'm Wren Traynor of Earth, recently a hijacker, computer whiz, and really, really tired."

Malax pulled her close, tucking her under his arm.

Borden's eyebrows rose higher. "I look forward to hearing the full story later, Wren." Her green gaze flicked back to Malax. "And War Commander, please thank your warrior Sassy for bringing us here. That woman deserves a pay raise."

Wren laughed and Malax just nodded. "Her work will be acknowledged."

They kept the comm line open and they watched the captain issuing orders to her crew. A second Kantos battlecruiser zeroed in on the *Divergent*.

Malax's jaw went tight. "The *Desteron*?"

"Five ship minutes out," Airen answered.

Come on, Thann-Eon. The last thing he wanted was for their Terran allies to be shot out of space. That would really put a dent in their new alliance.

"Repairs?" he asked.

"Are underway," a warrior replied. "All engineering crews are working to recover the engines."

"Sir, there is a Kantos kill squad on the hull of the Terran ship," Sabin called out.

Cren. "Let's see."

The viewscreen image zoomed in. Instantly, he saw the Kantos kill squad on the *Divergent*'s hull, trying to cut their way in.

Wren gasped. "Those fuckers."

"Can we fire on them?" Malax asked.

Sabin shook his head. "Not without a high risk of hitting the *Divergent*."

"Captain Borden," Malax said. "You have a Kantos kill squad attempting a breach." He waved a hand at his comms team. "Send her the images."

"We see them, War Commander." The captain sounded like she was preparing for a meal, calm and unruffled. "Lieutenant Park, engage the kill squad."

"About time," a deep, melodic female voice answered.

On screen, Malax watched an airlock on the Terran ship open. Several bodies streamed out, all wearing high-tech space suits and helmets.

"Space marines," Wren said.

Like her sister, Lara. He saw a close-up view of the female lieutenant leading her team. They arrowed straight toward the Kantos soldiers. He watched the space marines pull out long combat swords and engage the Kantos.

The fight was vicious and brutal. The Kantos were surprised, not expecting the attack.

Minutes later, the space marines had dispatched the entire Kantos kill squad.

"Wow," Wren said.

Wow, indeed. Malax glanced around the bridge, and saw all his warriors watching. Their expressions ranged from shock to awe.

Yes, the Eon had definitely underestimated the Terrans.

"Kantos battlecruiser is in range," a warrior said.

The ship looked enormous compared to the Terran ship.

"Malax." He heard the concern in Wren's voice.

He squeezed her fingers. "If there is one thing I've learned of late, it is not to underestimate the abilities of Terrans."

A smile flickered on her face.

"Fire on the battlecruiser," Captain Borden ordered. "Keep them off the *Rengard*."

"Airen, redirect the last of our fighters to aid the *Divergent*." Malax said.

On screen, he watched the *Divergent*'s marines flying back to the airlock.

"*Divergent*," Captain Borden said. "Let's show these bugs how we squish unwanted pests."

Boom. Boom. Boom.

Malax watched the *Divergent's* plasma weapons firing on the Kantos cruiser. They pounded the Kantos ship.

"That is enhanced weaponry," Sabin said, staring at the screen.

Airen moved up beside Malax. "Our scans show that once their plasma cannon is depleted, it'll take time to recharge."

The Kantos battlecruiser fired up its engines, moving in fast toward the Terran ship. His gut tightened.

"Are they going to ram the *Divergent*?" Wren said frantically.

"Sabin, keep that ship off them."

"Our main laser array is down," the security

commander answered. "They are just out of range of our remaining weapons."

Malax cursed. He couldn't just stand here and watch their allies be destroyed.

Suddenly, there was a burst of light. A large, sleek, black warship appeared beside the *Divergent*.

CHAPTER NINETEEN

W ren clapped her hands. She stared at the Eon warship and wanted to cheer and laugh.

"*Rengard*, this is the *Desteron*." War Commander Thann-Eon's face appeared on screen, framed by his brown hair.

"Did you take a scenic flight to get here?" Malax asked.

The war commander gave him a faint smile. "Looks like you didn't need us, anyway."

"No, we had some unexpected help," Malax said.

Thann-Eon turned to look at the uniformed man beside him. "Brack, work with the Terran ship. Take that battlecruiser down."

Beside Davion, his second-in-command nodded. He turned to face a console. "Terran ship *Divergent*, this is Second Commander Thann-Felis of the *Desteron*. Get out of our way and allow us to destroy the battlecruiser."

The *Divergent* was still firing. "We're doing just fine,

warrior," Captain Borden answered. "Get in line and stay out of *our* way."

Wren bit her lip. *Uh-oh.*

She watched the *Desteron* start firing on the battle-cruiser as well.

"*Divergent.*" Brack's voice held an annoyed edge. "We have the fire power to deal with the Kantos cruiser—"

"We already took one down," Borden shot back. "Alone. All by ourselves."

Brack growled.

Wren slapped a hand over her mouth and looked up at Malax. She saw her warrior was trying to keep a straight face.

"How about you fire on the cruiser's weapons?" Borden said. "Focus your fire there."

"I'm an Eon warrior, woman. I *give* orders, I don't take them."

"Not to my ship, warrior."

The *Divergent* moved, and kept firing on the battle-cruiser. A rain of Eon fighters flowed out of the side of the *Desteron*. They engaged the swarm ships, and more explosions lit up the viewscreen.

"Another warrior feels the sharp edge of a Terran female's tongue," Malax said.

"I thought you liked my tongue?" she shot back.

He smiled and his voice lowered. "I do."

Suddenly, Sassy's voice spoke up. "The Kantos are retreating. Or what's left of them."

The bridge of the *Rengard* erupted in elated cheers and whoops. The warriors' relief filled the room in a wave. Wren watched warriors hug and slap each other on the back. Nearby, Airen's shoulders slumped. The woman looked tired, but she was smiling. Sabin was watching the screen with a faint smile.

On-screen, Wren and Malax watched the *Desteron* and *Divergent* work together to chase off the last of the Kantos.

Terran and Eon. Together. Stronger.

Hope flooded Wren. Together, they had a chance to drive the Kantos away for good.

She looked up and Malax smiled down at her. Then, he pulled her up on her toes and kissed her, right in the middle of his bridge.

Allie

"TAKE OUT THAT LAST KANTOS SHIP," Captain Allie Borden ordered.

Her crew responded immediately, like the well-trained team they were. She felt the ship's engines vibrate under her feet as it shifted and took aim. It shuddered as their laser array fired.

She smiled. They were the best crew she'd worked with in her entire career, and the *Divergent* was the best ship she'd ever commanded.

Allie looked at the viewscreen, watching the scattering Kantos. *Run, you cowardly bugs.* Then her gaze fell on the *Desteron*.

While the *Divergent* was the best ship she'd

captained, she still had to admit that it was no Eon warship. God, that sleek, dark ship was pretty. Deadly and packed to the gills with high-tech weapons. *Mmm.*

Down, girl.

A laser blast hit the *Divergent's* shields, almost knocking her off her feet.

She spread her feet. "Li?"

"Shields holding, Captain."

A blast from the *Desteron* lit up the space in front of them. The intense ray of laser hit the Kantos ship, and a second later, the spacecraft exploded in a fiery ball.

She frowned and touched her earpiece. "Hey, Second Commander, you stole our kill."

"This is not a game, Captain." The deep rumble sounded a little pissed off.

Allie felt a spurt of satisfaction. Who knew that needling Eon warriors could be so much fun? She smiled again. When you spent most of your time in space, you had to find your fun wherever you could. Then her smile faded. Life was short, and you never knew how much time you had. It paid to enjoy it as much as you could.

"The Kantos warships are retreating, Captain," her comms officer called out.

"Let our fighters have them," Allie said. "Launch the squadron."

Her second-in-command, Sub-Captain Donovan Lennox nodded, folding his muscled arms over his chest. A second later, their fighters launched from the *Divergent.*

"We have a fire on Deck Seven," Donovan said.

Allie nodded. "Send the fire crew."

"Already inbound."

Ahead, she saw sexy, little Eon fighters slice through the darkness—the ships were sleek, with blue lights running up the sides of their streamlined forms.

"Captain, your fighters are welcome to join ours." Second Commander Thann-Felis' deep voice rumbled in her ear.

She rolled her eyes. "Your fighters are welcome to join *ours*. You were late to this fight, so you don't get to take over."

She heard snickers on her bridge and, with a frown, she shot a hard look around. The snickers died. She might enjoy needling the warrior and teaching him a little lesson in diplomacy, but she wouldn't allow insubordination on her bridge.

A second later, she wasn't surprised when the second commander drawled in her ear once more.

"Are you always this difficult, Captain?"

"No. Only when big, alien warriors try to boss me around."

"We're trying to *help*." He sounded like he was talking through gritted teeth.

"So, help, but don't try and take over."

Now Allie was pretty sure she could hear him grinding his teeth together. She glanced at Donovan, and the man was smiling, his teeth white against his dark skin.

She dropped into her captain's chair, swinging her personal comp screen up from the armrest. She swiped it and the image to go with the comm call appeared.

Her gut clenched. *Oh, hell.*

Of course, he had to be male perfection—a tough,

rugged face, with a sharp nose and strong jaw. Thick, brown hair brushed his jawline. She couldn't see all of his body, but she'd bet it matched the massive shoulders.

Down, girl.

"We have an alliance, Captain," he said. "I am not your enemy."

"Trust is earned, Second Commander."

"My name is Brack."

Brack. It suited him. Strong, a little gruff. "Look, Brack, you stay out of my way, and I'll stay out of yours."

The warrior smiled, and the air in Allie's chest tried to choke her. The smile turned him from rugged to handsome. She felt a flare of annoyance at the irritating attraction.

"I doubt we'll see very much of each other, Allie."

"That's Captain Borden, to you. And what, you think our inferior Terran ships won't keep up with yours?"

That smile widened. "You said it, not me...Captain."

The line closed, the screen turning black.

Ugh, men. Whatever the species, they all had the gene to drive a woman crazy.

Allie raised her voice. "Set a course back toward the *Rengard*. We'll dock with them on their starboard side."

"Yes, Captain."

Smoothly, the *Divergent* moved, reminding Allie why she loved being a starship captain. All that strength, power, and ability at her command. A team she trusted at her back.

A muted alarm started pinging.

"Captain?"

She glanced at her navigation officer. "Yes?"

"The *Desteron* is moving into that docking position."

Allie narrowed her eyes. *Asshole.* She knew he'd done that on purpose. "Adjust course."

Alliance or not, the second commander was proving to be extremely aggravating.

As the *Rengard* grew larger on the viewscreen, she settled back in her chair. Luckily, Brack Thann-Felis was the least of her problems and he was correct. She probably wouldn't ever see him again.

"Bring us in to dock, Lieutenant Harris." Right now, Allie was going to focus on her first chance to get aboard an Eon warship. Ships held much more interest to her than men.

THE DOORS to the *Rengard*'s bridge opened, and Eve and Lara Traynor strode in.

Malax heard Wren make a happy sound and break away from him. He watched as she was engulfed by her sisters. All three of them were hugging and talking at once.

Behind the women, Davion Thann-Eon and Caze Vann-Jad entered, watching their mates and smiling. Beside them, Davion's second-in-command, Brack, stood shaking his head and scowling.

Malax nodded at the warriors. "Welcome aboard the *Rengard.*"

"Glad you have your ship back under your command," Davion said.

Malax smiled. Actually, now that the situation was

nearing an end, he was pretty happy that Wren had hijacked his ship.

"You've sustained some damage," Brack said.

"Repairs are underway," Malax said. "We'd appreciate you staying until we have engines and weapons fully online."

Davion nodded. "Of course. I see the *Vymerion* arrived as well."

"Yes, War Commander Tynann-Ath agreed to patrol the outer perimeter."

The women broke apart. Wren looked at Malax and smiled. She rushed over to him, gripping his arm. "Eve, Lara, this is Malax."

Malax slid his arm around her shoulders and pulled her close. All the conversation ceased, and he saw looks being traded between Wren's sisters.

"You're mated," Eve said.

Lara's blue gaze narrowed on Malax.

Wren blinked. "What? Malax and I are...well, he's mine, now." She looked up at him and when she saw that he was smiling, her mouth dropped open. "Oh, God. Are we mated?"

Davion gripped Malax's shoulder. "Congratulations."

Malax pulled Wren in for a kiss. He rubbed his nose against hers. "I was waiting for all the excitement to die down before I told you. I knew the possessive pull I felt for you meant you were special. And when you shared my armor, my helian accepted you."

From nearby, Brack groaned. "Not another one."

"Don't scoff," Caze said. "You might find yourself an Earth woman, too, Brack."

Brack held a hand up. "No." He shook his head. "No. That is not happening."

Davion raised a dark brow. "You never know—"

"No," Brack said again. "They all drive you crazy."

Lara touched Caze's cheek, and the big warrior smiled. Eve bumped her hip against Davion's.

As far as Malax could tell, both men were very happy about their mated status.

"We wouldn't have it any other way," Davion confirmed.

"We're mated." Wren's voice was quiet. Then she grinned. "We're mated!"

She leaped on him and Malax caught her. "We are."

She wrapped her legs around his waist. "That means you're mine."

"Yes. And you're mine."

"This is wonderful news," Davion said.

Eve smiled at her sister. "You're happy?"

Wren nodded.

Then Davion's face turned serious. "We still need to deal with the Kantos."

Malax set Wren down. "We do."

"The king wants us to schedule a call with him," Davion said. "He's angry about this attack, and he wants a war plan. He wants to shut them down and drive them back into their own space."

Malax nodded. King Gayel Solann-Eon was head of the Eon Empire. He'd recently become king, ridding the Eon of lots of outdated edicts and rules, and was proving he was the right man for the job. Malax had a lot of respect for the warrior.

"And the king wants us to include our allies in our plans, and cement our alliance with Earth," Davion continued. "He'll be happy to hear of another Eon-Terran mating."

"I've found having Terrans aboard very useful." Malax stroked Wren's back. "Even when they're hijackers, kidnappers, or thieves."

Wren blushed, and her sisters both grinned.

"Captain Borden appears to be very skilled in space battles," Davion added.

From beside the war commander, Brack snorted.

"I'm going to recommend to King Gayel that he include the *Divergent* in our future planning," Davion added.

Brack's arms dropped to his sides. "What?"

Malax cleared his throat. "Well, I invited the captain aboard, so you can discuss it with her."

The doors to the bridge whispered open, and two women and a man stepped inside.

Malax took in the humans. They all wore deep-blue Space Corps uniforms, and had the straight bearing of people with military training.

Eve stepped forward. "Allie."

"Eve." The women hugged. "It's great to see you."

"You too. Heard you saved the day today."

Allie Borden smiled. "You know me, I like blowing things up." The *Divergent*'s captain turned to the group. "I'm Captain Allie Borden. This is my second, Sub-Captain Donovan Lennox." She gestured to the tall, dark-skinned man with a shaved head standing at her side. He was almost as tall as an Eon warrior.

The man nodded.

"And this is Lieutenant Jamie Park," Captain Borden continued.

Malax took one look at the tall, dark-haired woman eyeing them all with a hard look in her black eyes and knew the woman was dangerous. He knew without a doubt that she was the space marine he'd seen lead her team to decimate the Kantos kill squad on the *Divergent's* hull.

"I'm War Commander Malax Dann-Jad. It is a pleasure to have you aboard the *Rengard*. Your assistance today was greatly appreciated. We owe you our lives, Captain Borden."

He shook hands with the captain and found her grip firm and strong. Introductions were made between all the warriors and humans.

He noted the cool greeting between the captain and Brack.

Lara stepped forward. "Park, it's been awhile."

Jamie Park inclined her head, then pulled Lara in for a hard hug. "Lara Traynor." The women slapped each other on the back.

"Well, Lara Vann-Jad, now."

The other space marine shook her head. "Heard you tied yourself to an Eon warrior, and couldn't believe it." The woman eyed Caze. "Although, now I have a better understanding of why."

Malax stepped back, and noticed Brack scowling at Captain Borden. The woman was pointedly ignoring him.

"We're planning a meal to celebrate our win today," Malax said.

Wren smiled. "Excellent."

Suddenly, a flash of heat washed over Malax. As dizziness hit him, he thought he was going to stagger. He felt like his skin was burning.

"Malax?" Wren leaned into his side, looking up at him with a frown.

He grabbed her, pulling her closer. He wanted to feel her skin against his, and he wanted her away from all the other males in the room. Without thinking, he leaned down and sniffed her hair. He loved the scent of her.

Wren looked over at the others. "Something's wrong."

Caze and Davion were both smiling.

"It's the mating fever," Davion said.

Wren's sisters started smiling, too.

Malax needed to get his mate away from the bridge. Away from all the males surrounding her. He scooped her into his arms and she let out a gasp.

"Malax—"

"He'll be fine, Wren," Eve said. "In a day or two."

"I'm sorry to inform you that we will miss the dinner." Malax headed for the doors, calculating the quickest route to his cabin. "I'll be busy with my mate."

Wren's mouth dropped open, then she shivered, heat igniting in her eyes.

"Airen, take care of our guests." As soon as the doors closed, the only thing that existed for Malax was his mate.

She nipped his ear. "Hurry, my warrior."

CHAPTER TWENTY

"I'm almost there."

"Wren."

"I'm so close."

"*Cren*, get there."

Wren thrust her hips down, just as Malax bumped his up. She was filled with his thick cock, sensations firing all through her body. Her orgasm hit in a blinding rush.

She sank her nails into his chest, her back arching. She cried out his name.

"*By Eschar's embrace*, you're so tight." His voice was a deep growl. "All mine, my mate."

Wren threw her head back farther, her hands digging into his rock-hard pecs. A second later, he surged up, and flipped her onto her back.

He thrust inside her. "*Cren, cren*." Then he buried his face in her neck, his body surging into hers one last time. His hips bucked as he groaned through his release.

Malax rolled off her and collapsed on the bed. They were both breathing heavily.

She snuggled into him. After a full day of glorious, energetic, out-of-control sex, Wren felt pretty boneless, a little achy, and two hundred percent happy.

His hand sifted through her hair, and she pressed a kiss to his damp skin. "I love you, Malax."

"I love you too, *shara*."

She lifted her head and she saw the soft look on his rugged face.

"I know we haven't known each other long," she said. "And things got off to a rocky start. It's been a wild ride, but I'm crazy about you."

"Wren."

She snuggled closer. "I like your hot body, your bossiness—"

"I'm not bossy. It's called leadership."

She snorted. "I love your eyes, and the way you look out for me—"

"You need a protector," he said. "You have a habit of finding trouble."

She smacked his chest playfully. "I like that you like me for me. Just as I am."

His hand slid down her body and cupped her ass. "There are a lot of things about you to love."

"Well, I like everything about you. The way you keep your word, the way you talk about your family, how you care for your warriors. You're a good man, Malax Dann-Jad."

He rolled, pinning her beneath him. "And you're very cute."

Her nose wrinkled. "Women don't want to be cute, Malax. They want to be sexy, gorgeous—"

"You're those too, Wren Traynor. Or I should say Wren Dann-Jad."

Dann-Jad. They were mated. Just the look on his face was enough to make Wren a little teary.

He was everything she'd secretly wanted.

He kissed her nose. "I love that you care about everything and everyone. You do what's right, even when it's difficult. You love your sisters. You have a sweet, gorgeous ass—"

She rolled her eyes.

"Beautiful breasts." He cupped one.

"Malax!"

"I also love your smart brain." His thumb brushed across her lips. "I love all of you."

Wren let her legs fall open and felt his hard cock brush against her.

"Can you take me again?" he murmured.

"Oh, yes."

As he slid inside her, she did feel tender, but just like him, she was hungry again. He kissed her and Wren opened her mouth, kissing him back. She slid her hands into his thick hair. God, she loved his hair. She wrapped her legs around his hips and he started surging inside her.

The communicator beside the bed pinged.

"It's a call for Wren," Sassy's voice said.

Wren groaned. "Sassy, I—"

"Hey, sis." Eve's voice. "Just checking you're still alive."

Oh, God. Malax was deep inside her and her sister was on the line.

"Yes." She hoped Eve didn't notice that her voice was squeaky. "I'm good. Really good."

"I bet," Eve replied dryly.

Malax moved his hips, pulling out and thrusting back in. Wren bit down to stifle her moan and smacked his shoulder.

"Well, I drew the short straw to be the one to interrupt you guys." Eve's voice turned a little dreamy. "I remember how good the mating fever is."

Malax gave another firm thrust and Wren pressed the back of her head into the pillows. "Eve—"

"Right. Look, a call has been set up with King Gayel. You're both required."

"Oh," Wren managed.

Malax slid a hand between their bodies. A moment later, he was rolling her clit between his big fingers.

"We'll be there in ten minutes," Wren choked out, electric sensation arrowing through her.

"Twenty," Malax said.

Eve laughed. "See you soon. Have fun."

The call ended and Wren dug her nails into Malax's scalp. "Hurry."

MALAX STRODE THROUGH HIS SHIP, smiling. He was flanked by Airen and Sabin.

The *Rengard*'s repairs were progressing well. He was

mated and in love. His helian pulsed, and he felt very, very pleased.

He'd left Wren to get ready for the call with the king, and she'd been a little panicked, tearing through her clothing options.

Moments later, he stepped onto the bridge.

Ahead, Eve and Davion stood with Lara and Caze. A large creature was sniffing around Eve's feet. He frowned at the woolly, brown-and-white beast.

"Uh, that's Shaggy," Airen said. "Eve's...pet."

"Pet?"

Airen lowered her voice. "It's actually a synthesized beast from Hunter7. She...befriended it."

Malax shook his head. No one in Eon history had ever befriended one of the deadly creatures on the Eon's synthetic hunter planets. Unsurprisingly, he didn't find himself shocked that a Traynor sister had achieved this feat.

Captain Borden was also standing with the group. Her interesting blonde hair was pulled up in a high tail behind her head. Brack stood beside her with his brawny arms crossed over his chest.

The doors opened behind Malax and Wren rushed in, face flushed. She was fiddling with her curls.

"Do I look okay?" she asked.

"You look gorgeous. Why are you nervous?"

"I've never met a king before."

Malax tugged on a curl. "He's just a man."

She slapped his hand away. "Don't ruin my hair, I spent forever getting it right."

She quickly hugged her sisters. Then there was a

deep *woof*, and the canine leaped on her. The animal planted his front paws on Wren's chest and licked her face.

"Eek, you must be Shaggy," Wren said.

Malax stepped forward, ready to pull the animal away, but it dropped down on its own, tongue lolling.

Wren laughed and rubbed the dog's head. "Aren't you cute?"

Malax shook his head. Only Wren would think a deadly alien canine was cute.

"The king's call is coming through," Airen announced.

Turning, Malax watched the viewscreen change, and the face of the king of the Eon Empire appeared.

King Gayel Solann-Eon was a warrior's warrior, with broad shoulders and a powerful body. His aristocratic face held a sharp edge and he had the typical long, brown hair of an Eon warrior. He wore a sleeveless shirt in a rich blue, and a gold cord circled one of his biceps.

"I'm very happy to hear that everyone is okay," the king said.

"Thank you, your majesty," Davion said.

"*That's* your king," Wren whispered. "He looks like a movie star."

The king's gaze moved to Captain Borden. "And thank you, Captain Borden, for your timely assistance."

The woman nodded. "Happy to help."

The king's gaze moved back to Malax and Davion. "I hear the Kantos have been driven off."

"For now," Malax said. "But they'll be scheming."

King Gayel nodded. "And all the *Rengard's* helians

have been secured...except one."

Clearing her throat, Wren stepped forward and gave a pained smile. "Um, about Sassy—"

"I've been briefed," the king said with a faint smile. "So, you're the Traynor sister who hijacked my warship?"

Wren shot her sisters a wide-eyed look before she turned back to the screen. "Um...sorry?"

Malax stepped forward and rested his hand on her shoulder. "I would like to introduce Wren, your majesty. She is also my mate."

The king blinked. "Another warrior mated to a Terran?"

Malax and Wren shared a smile. "Yes."

"I'm pleased for you, War Commander," King Gayel said.

"I request that Wren join me on the *Rengard*. She's talented with tech and computers, and she's linked with Sassy. Without her intervention, the *Rengard* would have been lost long before Captain Borden and the *Divergent* arrived."

Captain Borden frowned. "Wait? Sassy, the woman who brought my ship here, isn't a warrior?"

Wren shook her head. "Sassy is a helian that absorbed my tablet and bonded with me."

"It sounds very advantageous to our alliance." The king sat back. "I'll be very happy for Wren to work with our helians, and see if there's anything we can gain from Terran technology. It seems that we've been writing off Terran technology for too long."

Wren smiled, looking radiant. "I would *love* that."

The king smiled too. "Good. I believe we should test

the link you have with Sassy, see how that link could be enhanced."

"Cool," Wren breathed.

"I agree," Sassy's voice came from Wren's wristband.

"Malax," the king said. "I've been told you encountered some interesting and powerful ancient tech on the planet you and Wren crash-landed on?"

"Yes. I definitely think we should investigate it. There could be useful weaponry."

"Very good. I'll assign that work to a science vessel." Gayel nodded. "I also have many more plans to strengthen our alliance with Earth. Ambassador?"

Eve wrinkled her nose. "I've asked you not to call me that, your majesty."

Malax raised a brow. Apparently, Eve had no trouble talking frankly with the Eon king. Although, something made him suspect that the Traynor sisters spoke frankly to everyone, regardless of rank or position.

"You've been making plans as we discussed?" Gayel asked.

Eve nodded. "Yes. I've put together a plan for training exercises between the Eon fleet and Space Corps."

Brack straightened as though he'd been stung by a Kantos bug. "What?"

"The king wants to strengthen the tactics we all use against the Kantos," Davion said. "Captain Borden, we'd like you and your ship to work with the *Desteron* and her crew."

The captain gave a slight jolt, her face carefully blank. "Great."

"You can coordinate with my second," Davion said.

The captain managed a nod, not looking at Brack. "Wonderful."

"I'm working on other ways to help ensure our alliance stays healthy and strong," the king added. "I'll be inviting a delegation from Earth to visit my palace here on Eon." Then the man's face turned serious, and it was easy to see the warrior he'd been before he'd ascended to the throne. "We will take the necessary steps to learn from each other and strengthen our alliance. Together we will take down the Kantos."

"Well, we've already done our bit for Eon-Terran relations," Wren murmured.

Malax leaned down, his lips brushing hers. The two of them had already forged a bond that was closer than any alliance.

"AND THEN HE scowled at me, all grumpy and bossy, and said—" Eve lowered her voice to a deep rumble "—'Eve, if I wasn't in love with you, I'd have you chained up in my brig.'"

Wren and Lara burst out laughing. Wren wrapped her arm around her belly, happiness fizzing in her blood. It was so good to spend time with her sisters.

The three of them were together in the dining room on the *Rengard*. Meal time was over, so they had the place to themselves. They were relaxed, happy, and without any immediate disasters looming over their heads.

For so long, it had just been the three of them against the world. Now, everything had changed for the better.

"God, I'm still starving." Eve picked at the last remnants of the sweet cakes on the dessert plate. She'd already mowed through several of them.

Wren reached out and grabbed Eve's hand, then Lara's. "I'm so glad you're both okay. Better than okay."

"Not that long ago, I was locked in prison, certain my life was over." Eve smiled. "And here I am, happier than I've ever been." Her nose wrinkled. "Except when people keep on addressing me as *ambassador*."

"You *are* an ambassador," Lara said.

Eve pointed. "Say that again and I'll punch you."

Lara popped a small fruit in her mouth. "You could try, little sister."

Used to the byplay, Wren grinned.

"I am so damn thrilled for my sisters," Eve said. "Everything worked out. Better than I ever imagined."

"Amen, sister." Lara's blue gaze landed on Wren. "Your warrior's treating you right?"

Wren felt heat in her cheeks. "Oh, yeah." Especially in their bed, wrapped up in each other's arms. "He's amazing."

"You're sure?" Lara said.

Wren huffed out a breath, used to overprotective older sisters. "Just because I'm not a badass space marine doesn't mean I can't handle an Eon warrior. Believe me, I handle him just fine."

"I don't think she's talking about on the bridge." Eve shoved another bite of cake in her mouth and waggled her eyebrows.

"No sex talk," Lara groaned. "Wren's the baby. I can't handle it.'"

Wren smiled. "He loves me, just as I am. My body, my brain, my smart mouth."

Her sisters both smiled.

Eve gripped Wren's arm and squeezed. "Good."

Lara nodded. "I won't murder him in his sleep, then."

"Incoming warrior alert." Sassy's voice came from Wren's wristband.

"Thanks, Sassy," Wren said.

Eve eyed her wrist. "I like your new friend."

"Me, too."

"And I like being one of the girls," Sassy added.

Lara rolled her eyes, but was smiling.

The dining room doors slid open and their warriors strolled in.

Oh, wow. Every time Wren saw Malax, her heart went pitty-pat. She suspected it would still happen even when they were old and gray.

She remembered when this had all started, when she'd first hijacked the *Rengard*, how she'd thought the warriors all looked the same. Now, they all seemed so different. Of course, they were all impossibly hot, sexy, and gorgeous.

"We are so damn lucky." Wren's eyes locked with Malax's.

"We sure are," Eve agreed.

"Captain Borden returned to the *Divergent*," Davion said. "They'll rendezvous with the *Desteron* in a week for the training exercises."

"Allie is top-notch," Eve said. "She's a damn good

captain." Then Eve pressed her tongue to her teeth. "Brack seemed...less than thrilled with his upcoming exercises."

"I got the same feeling from Allie," Lara said.

"He will do as ordered," Davion said.

Suddenly, Eve and Lara rose.

"So, Malax..." Eve began.

As her sisters converged on her man, Wren stiffened.

"We want assurances that you're going to take care of our baby sister," Lara said silkily.

Wren scowled. "Hey, I'm an adult—"

"We want assurances you'll put her happiness and wellbeing first," Eve said.

"Hel-*lo*." Wren threw her hands in the air. "Fully grown woman here."

Davion and Caze looked amused, crossing their brawny arms over their chests.

"We could take you," Lara said in a tone that raised goosebumps on Wren's arms.

"No, you couldn't," Malax said. "But there's no need to test that theory. I want nothing but Wren's happiness. I'll do everything in my power to ensure it."

Wren melted. "Malax—"

Black-gold eyes met hers. "I'd die for her."

She moved straight to him, burying her face in his chest. "I'd prefer you didn't die."

"I love you, Wren. As do your sisters. You will always belong with me, by my side, in my arms, and in my heart."

Happy tears welled in her eyes. "Don't make me cry."

"It's the truth. Remember, a war commander never—"

"Lies. I remember." She went up on her toes and pressed her mouth to his.

Nearby, she heard a sniffle. She pulled back and froze. Eve had tears in her eyes. Her tough-as-nails sister *never* cried.

"Don't mind me..." Eve waved a hand in the air. "Clearly my war commander is making me soft."

Davion slid an arm around her.

"Actually," Sassy interjected. "According to my scans, your war commander has impregnated you."

Silence. Wren just stared.

Eve's eyes grew bigger and bigger.

"I believe the hormones are affecting your appetite and your emotions," Sassy added cheerfully.

"What?" Eve breathed.

Lara looked shocked, and Wren slapped a hand over her mouth. Davion stood, frozen like a statue.

"You're lying." There was panic in Eve's voice.

Sassy sniffed. "I don't lie."

Davion slid a hand down his mate's belly, spreading his fingers out. Wren felt a pulse in the air and knew it came from his helian.

Then the war commander's eyes went wide and a smile broke out on his face. *"By Eschar's bow*, Eve, you carry our babe."

Eve spun to face him. "You got me pregnant!"

"Calm yourself, *shara*."

"This is something we discuss, first."

He pulled her into his arms. "It happens with mates. I've never been mated, and didn't give it any thought."

Lara stiffened. "What?" She elbowed Caze. "One day, warrior, but not today."

The security commander shrugged a shoulder. "The helian controls fertility."

Lara's eyes widened. "I'm going to see Aiden. I need birth control, stat."

"One day, I'd like to see you swollen with our child," Caze said.

Wren watched her tough sister smile. "You would be a wonderful daddy."

Nearby, Davion's head was bent close to Eve's.

"I don't know how to be a mother," Eve said. "I know how to kick ass, not take care of kids. My mother wasn't a very good role model."

"Eve, you're a loving, amazing woman," Davion said. "You helped raise your sisters. You take good care of Shaggy."

"I've seen Shaggy lick his own poop. I don't think that's a good thing."

Davion cupped her face. "You'll be a fierce and amazing mother to our child."

Eve pulled in a breath and it seemed to steady her. "A baby. Our baby." Wonder crossed her face. "A bit of you and a bit of me."

Davion kissed her.

"I'm so freaking happy," Wren said.

"Me too," Sassy whispered.

Malax pulled Wren close and tightened his arms. "As am I. I finally caught my little hijacker, and have her right where I want her."

Wren breathed him in and realized she was right where she belonged.

I hope you enjoyed Wren and Malax's story!

Eon Warriors continues with *Kiss of Eon* starring Second Commander Brack Thann-Felis as he collides with Earth woman, Captain Allie Borden. Coming later in 2019.

For more action-packed romance, read on for a preview of the first chapter of *Gladiator,* the first book in my best-selling Galactic Gladiators series.

Don't miss out! For updates about new releases, action romance info, free books, and other fun stuff, sign up for my VIP mailing list and get your *free box set* containing three action-packed romances.

Visit here to get started: www.annahackettbooks.com

FREE BOX SET DOWNLOAD

JOIN THE ACTION-PACKED ADVENTURE!

PREVIEW: GLADIATOR

MORE SCI-FI ROMANCE

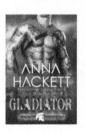

Fighting for love, honor, and freedom on the galaxy's lawless outer rim.

Fighting for love, honor, and freedom on the galaxy's lawless outer rim...

When Earth space marine Harper Adams finds herself abducted by alien slavers off a space station, her life turns into a battle for survival. Dumped into an arena on a desert planet on the outer rim, she finds herself face to face with a big, tattooed alien gladiator...the champion of the Kor Magna Arena.

Just another day at the office.

Harper Adams pulled herself along the outside of the space station module. She could hear her quiet breathing inside her spacesuit, and she easily pulled her weightless body along the slick, white surface of the module. She stopped to check a security panel, ensuring all the systems were running smoothly.

Check. Same as it had been yesterday, and the day before that. But Harper never ever let herself forget that they were six hundred million kilometers away from Earth. That meant they were dependent only on themselves. She tapped some buttons on the security panel before closing the reinforced plastic cover. She liked to dot all her *I*s and cross all her *T*s. She never left anything to chance.

She grabbed the handholds and started pulling herself up over the cylindrical pod to check the panels on the other side. Glancing back behind herself, she caught a beautiful view of the planet below.

Harper stopped and made herself take it all in. The orange, white, and cream bands of Jupiter could take your breath away. Today, she could even see the famous superstorm of the Great Red Spot. She'd been on the Fortuna Research Station for almost eighteen months. That meant, despite the amazing view, she really didn't see it anymore.

She turned her head and looked down the length of the space station. At the end was the giant circular donut that housed the main living quarters and offices. The main ring rotated to provide artificial gravity for the residents. Lying off the center of the ring was the long cylinder of the research facility, and off that cylinder were several modules that housed various scientific labs and storage. At the far end of the station was the docking area for the supply ships that came from Earth every few months.

"Lieutenant Adams? Have you finished those checks?"

Harper heard the calm voice of her fellow space marine and boss, Captain Samantha Santos, through the comm system in her helmet.

"Almost done," Harper answered.

"Take a good look at the botany module. The computer's showing some strange energy spikes, but the scientists in there said everything looks fine. Must be a system malfunction."

Which meant the geek squad engineers were going to have to come in and do some maintenance. "On it."

Harper swung her body around, and went feet-first down the other side of the module. She knew the rest of the security team—all made up of United Nations Space Marines—would be running similar checks on the other modules across the station. They had a great team to ensure the safety of the hundreds of scientists aboard the station. There was also a dedicated team of engineers that kept the guts of the station running.

She passed a large, solid window into the module, and could see various scientists floating around benches filled with all kinds of plants. They all wore matching gray jumpsuits accented with bright-blue at the collars, that indicated science team. There was a vast mix of scientists and disciplines aboard—biologists, botanists, chemists, astronomers, physicists, medical experts, and the list went on. All of them were conducting experiments, and some were searching for alien life beyond the edge of the solar system. It seemed like every other week, more probes were being sent out to hunt for radio signals or collect samples.

Since humans had perfected large solar sails as a way to safely and quickly propel spacecraft, getting around the solar system had become a lot easier. With radiation pressure exerted by sunlight onto the mirrored sails, they could travel from Earth to Fortuna Station orbiting Jupiter in just a few months. And many of the scientists aboard the station were looking beyond the solar system, planning manned expeditions farther and farther away. Harper wasn't sure they were quite ready for that.

She quickly checked the adjacent control panel. Among all the green lights, she spotted one that was blinking red, and she frowned. They definitely had a problem with the locking system on the exterior door at the end of the module. She activated the small propulsion pack on her spacesuit, and circled around the module. She slowed down as she passed the large, round exterior door at the end of the cylindrical module.

It was all locked into place and looked secure.

As she moved back to the module, she grabbed a handhold and then tapped the small tablet attached to the forearm of her suit. She keyed in a request for maintenance to come and check it.

She looked up and realized she was right near

another window. Through the reinforced glass, a pretty, curvy blonde woman looked up and spotted Harper. She smiled and waved. Harper couldn't help but smile and lifted her gloved hand in greeting.

Dr. Regan Forrest was a botanist and a few years younger than Harper. The young woman was so open and friendly, and had befriended Harper from her first day on the station. Harper had never had a lot of friends —mainly because she'd been too busy raising her younger sister and working. She'd never had time for girly nights out or gossip.

But Regan was friendly, smart, and had the heart of a steamroller under her pretty exterior. Harper always had trouble saying no to her. Maybe the woman reminded her a little of Brianna. At the thought of her sister, something twisted painfully in Harper's chest.

Regan floated over to the window and held up a small tablet. She'd typed in some words.

Cards tonight?

Harper had been teaching Regan how to play poker. The woman was terrible at it, and Harper beat her all the time. But Regan never gave up.

Harper nodded and held up two fingers to indicate a couple of hours. She was off-shift shortly, and then she had a sparring match with Regan's cousin, Rory—one of the station engineers—in the gym. Aurora "Call me Rory or I'll hit you" Fraser had been trained in mixed martial arts, and Harper found the female engineer a hell of a sparring partner. Rory was teaching Harper some martial arts moves and Harper was showing the woman some basic sword moves. Since she was little, Harper had been a keen fencer.

Regan grinned back and nodded. Then the woman's wide smile disappeared. She spun around, and through the glass Harper could see the other scientists all looking around, concerned. One scientist was spinning around, green plants floating in the air around him, along with fat droplets of water and some other green fluid. He'd clearly screwed up and let his experiment get free.

"Lieutenant Adams?" The captain's voice came through her helmet again. "Harper?"

There was a sense of urgency that made Harper's belly tighten. "Go ahead, Captain."

"We have an alarm sounding in the botany module. The computer says there is a risk of decompression."

Dammit. "I just checked the security panels. The locking mechanism on the exterior door is showing red. I did a visual inspection and it's closed up tight."

"Okay, we talked with the scientist in charge. Looks like one of her team let something loose in there. It isn't dangerous, but it must be messing with the alarm sensors. System's locked them all in there." She made an annoyed sound. "Idiots will have to stay there until engineering can get down there and free them."

Harper studied the room through the glass again. Some of the green liquid had floated over to another bench that contained various frothing cylinders on it. A second later, the cylinders shattered, their contents bubbling upward.

The scientists all moved to the back exit of the

module, banging on the locked door. *Damn*. They were trapped.

Harper met Regan's gaze. Her friend's face was pale, and wisps of her blonde hair had escaped her ponytail, floating around her face.

"Captain," Harper said. "Something's wrong. The experiments have overflowed their containment." She could see the scientists were all coughing.

"Engineering is on the way," the captain said.

Harper pushed herself off, flying over the surface of the module. She reached the control panel and saw that several other lights had turned red. They needed to get this under control and they needed to do it now.

"Harper!" The captain's panicked voice. "Decompression in progress!"

What the hell? The module jerked beneath Harper. She looked up and saw the exterior door blow off, flying away from the station.

Her heart stopped. That meant all the scientists were exposed to the vacuum of space.

Fuck. Harper pushed off again, sending herself flying toward the end of the module. She put her arms by her sides to help increase her speed. Through the window, she saw that most of the scientists had grabbed on to whatever they could hold on to. A few were pulling emergency breathers over their heads.

She reached the end of the pod and saw the damage. There was torn metal where the door had been ripped off. Inside the door, she knew there would be a temporary repair kit containing a sheet of high-tech nano fabric that could be stretched across the opening to reestablish pressure. But it needed to be put in place manually. Harper reached for the latch to release the repair kit.

Suddenly, a slim body shot out of the pod, her arms and legs kicking. Her mouth was wide open in a silent scream.

Regan. Harper didn't let herself think. She turned, pushed off and fired her propulsion system, arrowing after her friend.

"Security Team to the botany module," she yelled through her comm system. "Security Team to botany module. We have decompression. One scientist has been expelled. I'm going after her. I need someone that can help calm the others and get the module sealed again."

"Acknowledged, Lieutenant," Captain Santos answered. "I'm on my way."

Harper focused on reaching Regan. She was gaining on her. She saw that the woman had lost consciousness. She also knew that Regan had only a couple of minutes to survive out here. Harper let her training take over. She tapped the propulsion system controls, trying for more speed, as she maneuvered her way toward Regan.

As she got close, Harper reached out and wrapped her arm around the scientist. "I've got you."

Harper turned, at the same time clipping a safety line to the loops on Regan's jumpsuit. Then, she touched the controls and propelled them straight back towards the module. She kept her friend pulled tightly toward her chest. *Hold on, Regan.*

She was so still. It reminded Harper of holding Brianna's dead body in her arms. Harper's jaw tightened. She wouldn't let Regan die out here. The woman had dreamed of working in space, and worked her entire career to get here, even defying her family. Harper wasn't going to fail her.

As the module got closer, she saw that the security team had arrived. She saw the captain's long, muscled body as she and another man put up the nano fabric.

"Incoming. Keep the door open."

"Can't keep it open much longer, Adams," the captain replied. "Make it snappy."

Harper adjusted her course, and, a second later, she shot through the door with Regan in her arms. Behind her, the captain and another huge security marine, Lieutenant Blaine Strong, pulled the stretchy fabric across the opening.

"Decompression contained," the computer intoned.

Harper released a breath. On the panel beside the door, she saw the lights turning green. The nano fabric wouldn't hold forever, but it would do until they got everyone out of here, and then got a maintenance team in here to fix the door.

"Oxygen levels at required levels," the computer said again.

"Good work, Lieutenant." Captain Sam Santos floated over. She was a tall woman with a strong face and brown hair she kept pulled back in a tight ponytail. She had curves she kept ruthlessly toned, and golden skin she always said was thanks to her Puerto Rican heritage.

"Thanks, Captain." Harper ripped her helmet off and looked down at Regan.

Her blonde hair was a wild tangle, her face was pale and marked by what everyone who worked in space called space hickeys—bruises caused by the skin's small blood vessels bursting when exposed to the vacuum of space. *Please be okay.*

"Here." Blaine appeared, holding a portable breather. The big man was an excellent marine. He was about six foot five with broad shoulders that stretched his spacesuit to the limit. She knew he was a few inches over the height limit for space operations, but he was a damn good marine, which must have gone in his favor. He had dark skin thanks to his African-American father and his handsome face made him popular with the station's single ladies, but mostly he worked and hung out with the other marines.

"Thanks." Harper slipped the clear mask over Regan's mouth.

"Nice work out there." Blaine patted her shoulder. "She's alive because of you."

Suddenly, Regan jerked, pulling in a hard breath.

"You're okay." Harper gripped Regan's shoulder. "Take it easy."

Regan looked around the module, dazed and panicky. Harper watched as Regan caught sight of the fabric stretched across the end of the module, and all the plants floating around inside.

"God," Regan said with a raspy gasp, her breath fogging up the dome of the breather. She shook her head, her gaze moving to Harper. "Thanks, Harper."

"Any time." Harper squeezed her friend's shoulder. "It's what I'm here for."

Regan managed a wan smile. "No, it's just you. You

didn't have to fly out into space to rescue me. I'm grateful."

"Come on. We need to get you to the infirmary so they can check you out. Maybe put some cream on your hickeys."

"Hickeys?" Regan touched her face and groaned. "Oh, no. I'm going to get a ribbing."

"And you didn't even get them the pleasurable way."

A faint blush touched Regan's cheeks. "That's right. If I had, at least the ribbing would have been worth it."

With a relieved laugh, Harper looked over at her captain. "I'm going to get Regan to the infirmary."

The other woman nodded. "Good. We'll meet you back at the Security Center."

With a nod, Harper pushed off, keeping one arm around Regan, and they floated into the main part of the science facility. Soon, they moved through the entrance into the central hub of the space station. As the artificial gravity hit, Harper's boots thudded onto the floor. Beside her, Regan almost collapsed.

Harper took most of the woman's weight and helped her down the corridor. They pushed into the infirmary.

A gray-haired, barrel-chested man rushed over. "Decided to take an unscheduled spacewalk, Dr. Forrest?"

Regan smiled weakly. "Yes. Without a spacesuit."

The doctor made a tsking sound and then took her from Harper. "We'll get her all patched up."

Harper nodded. "I'll come and check on you later."

Regan grabbed her hand. "We have a blackjack game

scheduled. I'm planning to win back all those chocolates you won off me."

Harper snorted. "You can try." It was good to see some life back in Regan's blue eyes.

As Harper strode out into the corridor, she ran a hand through her dark hair, tension slowly melting out of her shoulders. She really needed a beer. She tilted her neck one way and then the other, hearing the bones pop.

Just another day at the office. The image of Regan drifting away from the space station burst in her head. Harper released a breath. She was okay. Regan was safe and alive. That was all that mattered.

With a shake of her head, Harper headed toward the Security Center. She needed to debrief with the captain and clock off. Then she could get out of her spacesuit and take the one-minute shower that they were all allotted.

That was the one thing she missed about Earth. Long, hot showers.

And swimming. She'd been a swimmer all her life and there were days she missed slicing through the water.

She walked along a long corridor, meeting a few people—mainly scientists. She reached a spot where there was a long bank of windows that afforded a lovely view of Jupiter, and space beyond it.

Stingy showers and unscheduled spacewalks aside, Harper had zero regrets about coming out into space. There'd been nothing left for her on Earth, and to her surprise, she'd made friends here on Fortuna.

As she stared out into the black, mesmerized by the twinkle of stars, she caught a small flash of light in the distance. She paused, frowning. What the hell was that?

She stared hard at the spot where she'd seen the flash. Nothing there but the pretty sprinkle of stars. Harper shook her head. Fatigue was playing tricks on her. It had to have just been a weird trick of the lights reflecting off the glass.

Pushing the strange sighting away, she continued on to the Security Center.

Galactic Gladiators

Gladiator

Warrior

Hero

Protector

Champion

Barbarian

Beast

Rogue

Guardian

Cyborg

Imperator

Also Available as Audiobooks!

READY FOR ANOTHER?

**IN THE AFTERMATH OF
AN ALIEN INVASION:**

**HEROES WILL RISE...
WHEN THEY HAVE
SOMEONE TO LIVE FOR**

In the aftermath of a deadly alien invasion, a band of survivors fights on...

In a world gone to hell, Elle Milton—once the darling of the Sydney social scene—has carved a role for herself as the communications officer for the toughest commando team fighting for humanity's survival—Hell Squad. It's her chance to make a difference and make up for horrible past mistakes...despite the fact that its battle-hardened commander never wanted her on his team.

When Hell Squad is tasked with destroying a strategic alien facility, Elle knows they need her skills in the field. But first she must go head to head with Marcus Steele and convince him she won't be a liability.

Marcus Steele is a warrior through and through. He fights to protect the innocent and give the human race a chance to survive. And that includes the beautiful, gutsy Elle who twists him up inside with a single look. The last thing he wants is to take her into a warzone, but soon they are thrown together battling both the alien invaders and their overwhelming attraction. And Marcus will learn just how much he'll sacrifice to keep her safe.

Hell Squad

Marcus

Cruz

Gabe

Reed

Roth

Noah

Shaw

Holmes

Niko

Finn

Theron

Hemi

Ash

Levi

Manu

Griff

Also Available as Audiobooks!

ALSO BY ANNA HACKETT

Team 52

Mission: Her Protection

Mission: Her Rescue

Mission: Her Security

Mission: Her Defense

Also Available as Audiobooks!

Treasure Hunter Security

Undiscovered

Uncharted

Unexplored

Unfathomed

Untraveled

Unmapped

Unidentified

Undetected

Also Available as Audiobooks!

Eon Warriors

Edge of Eon

Touch of Eon

Also Available as Audiobooks!

Galactic Gladiators

Also Available as Audiobooks!

Hell Squad

Niko

Finn

Theron

Hemi

Ash

Levi

Manu

Griff

Also Available as Audiobooks!

The Anomaly Series

Time Thief

Mind Raider

Soul Stealer

Salvation

Anomaly Series Box Set

The Phoenix Adventures

Among Galactic Ruins

At Star's End

In the Devil's Nebula

On a Rogue Planet

Beneath a Trojan Moon

Beyond Galaxy's Edge

On a Cyborg Planet

Return to Dark Earth

On a Barbarian World

Lost in Barbarian Space

Through Uncharted Space

Crashed on an Ice World

Perma Series

Winter Fusion

A Galactic Holiday

Warriors of the Wind

Tempest

Storm & Seduction

Fury & Darkness

Standalone Titles

Savage Dragon

Hunter's Surrender

One Night with the Wolf

For more information visit AnnaHackettBooks.com

ABOUT THE AUTHOR

I'm a USA Today bestselling author and I'm passionate about ***action romance***. I love stories that combine the thrill of falling in love with the excitement of action, danger and adventure. I'm a sucker for that moment when the team is walking in slow motion, shoulder-to-shoulder heading off into battle. I write about people overcoming unbeatable odds and achieving seemingly impossible goals. I like to believe it's possible for all of us to do the same.

My books are mixture of action, adventure and sexy romance and they're recommended for anyone who enjoys fast-paced stories where the boy wins the girl at the end (or sometimes the girl wins the boy!)

For release dates, action romance info, free books, and other fun stuff, sign up for the latest news here:

Website: www.annahackettbooks.com

Made in the USA
Coppell, TX
27 November 2020

42196738R00146